In The Cold, Cradled Ground

A Jack Sullivan Mystery

By

William G. Krejci

Author's Note:

Although this story takes place in the greater Cleveland area, I have used fictional street names and communities in scenes where violent crimes occur.

For my friends at McNamara's.

Chapter 1

Shelby Tomlinson was 14 years old. She stood just shy of five and a half feet tall and had long brown hair and bright blue eyes. Most of the boys at school considered her pretty, but not extraordinary. She wasn't very athletic nor did she have any interest in cheer leading. Those were the girls that really attracted the boys' attention. Shelby wasn't interested in any of this though. She'd much rather hang out with her friends after school than involve herself in extra curricular activities.

Jayna was Shelby's newest friend. They hadn't associated much throughout junior high, but now that they were high school freshmen, and found themselves in many classes together, they began to learn that they had much in common. Both were big fans of Nirvana and occasionally liked to skip class to catch a smoke. Jayna had been taken under the wings of a sophomore named Sandy and had been brought into the clique of the quote-unquote stoner chicks... even though none of them had ever smoked pot. Within the week, Shelby had joined their ranks.

September had been unusually warm, but as October of 1992 wore on, the weather had taken a chilly turn. Shelby began to wear thermal shirts more often under her tees and eventually started to rip out small holes by the cuffs to pass her thumbs through. Her mother had given her a denim jacket for her birthday the previous November, but Shelby never really cared to wear it. Mid-October meant brisk mornings and cool evenings. Shelby would leave the house with the jacket along with a promise to her mother that she would wear it, though she hardly ever would. It wasn't until one morning that Sandy saw her wearing it that the jacket became interesting. Sandy came up behind her with a purple art marker and inscribed a quick doodle of a skull on the shoulder. After that, Shelby's denim jacket became a wearable piece of art. Everyone began to put something on it; be it a picture or a signature. Shelby now wore the jacket everyday.

On the evening of October 17th, Shelby was walking home from Jayna's house, hoping to be home in time for dinner. She'd been late once already that week and her mom had berated her for over an hour. It was just Shelby and her mom now. Her father had left them four years earlier and was now living in a small suburb outside of Cincinnati with his new wife and two-year-old son. She felt bad when she was late because she knew that her mother had no one else. She'd stayed at Jayna's a little longer than she should have and knew that she'd have to make up for the lost time on the way home.

Shelby was walking at a brisk pace through the suburban neighborhood under the failing light of the shortening days. She'd been walking for about five minutes before she noticed the sound of a car with a bad exhaust slowly following behind her. She stopped and turned, half expecting it to be her mother, but instantly noticed that the headlights were quite different. The car behind her was in fact a black, mid-80's model, Ford LTD. Her mother drove a Honda, a much smaller vehicle, but with an equally noisy exhaust. She couldn't get a good look at the driver, but could tell that it was a man in a baseball cap. The man was peering out his passenger-side window and was shining a flashlight up the driveway he was stopped at the end of. Shelby began to walk again, this time even quicker than she had been. As she did, the car slowly accelerated to match her pace. Glancing over her shoulder, she saw the man again stop and shine a flashlight up the next driveway. She continued to walk.

"I'm sorry miss, but could you help me?"

Shelby turned to find herself blinded by an intense light coming from the LTD.

"Oh, I'm sorry," the man said as he lowered his flashlight. Though she couldn't see his face, Shelby could tell that the man was somewhere in his early forties or so and was wearing some sort of a uniform that included a button-up shirt and a matching hat. "I'm new to the area and am trying to locate 3198 Laurelwood Avenue."

Shelby cautiously approached the car in hopes of getting a better look at the man. She still couldn't see his face too clearly, but now saw that he had a goatee and was wearing a pizza delivery uniform.

"You're on Lynnwood Drive," she explained. "Laurelwood is seven blocks west of here."

"Is that so?" the man replied as he took a darting look about

8

him.

"Yeah, a bit confusing I guess," she continued. "If you go up here to Mapledale and hang a left, it should be on your left-hand side."

"Well thank you very much. Like I said, I'm new here and I'm still trying to get my bearings."

"I'm sure you'll figure it out."

Shelby was about to step away from the LTD and continue on home when the driver asked her another question.

"So, what's your name?"

Shelby thought better of it.

"Um... Samantha", she lied. "Samantha Young."

"Well, Um Samantha... Samantha Young, thank you again for your help. I only hope that everyone else in this town is as nice as you are."

Shelby was flattered by the compliment, but was trying to make it clear that she needed to be on her way. Besides, there seemed to be something slightly off with the man in the car. He was coming off as overly anxious for some reason. A moment later, she realized why.

"Say, I've got an idea. Seeing as I'm not familiar with the neighborhood, I could definitely use a navigator."

Shelby took a step back.

"I'd be willing to split my tips fifty-fifty," he offered.

"That's okay," Shelby replied. "Besides, I need to get home for dinner."

"Dinner? The benefit of delivering pizza is that it's also an all-you-can-eat buffet."

"Really, my mother's expecting me."

"Well how about a ride home then?"

Shelby took another step back. She suddenly realized what it was that had been bothering her. This man had claimed to be a pizza deliveryman, yet there was no smell of pizza to speak of coming from his car. She should have been able to catch at least the faintest aroma of cheese or pepperoni or even tomato sauce, but there was nothing: only the smell of stale cigarettes and some strange chemical that she couldn't quite place.

"Laurelwood is seven blocks west of here," she said directly and to the point. "You have a good evening now."

Shelby was frightened out of her wits. She turned and nervously proceeded down Lynnwood Drive at a much faster pace than she had walked all night. She was readying herself to break into a run if needed. She stiffened and glanced over her shoulder to see the LTD still sitting where she had left it. As she turned her head forward again, she heard it suddenly accelerate, but continue on past her to the end of the block. The car turned left at Mapledale. She stopped and breathed a sigh of relief as it did.

As Shelby continued homeward, she kept playing out in her mind what had just transpired. She was no longer as concerned about being late as she had been. The man in the car now consumed her every thought. She now wondered if she should tell her mother about this. Her mother, she thought, might get angry with her for talking to a stranger. She might not even let her go over to Jayna's house after dark anymore. She'd definitely tell the girls at school about it. They might even think of her as something of a hero for having talked off this creep. It was both frightening and exciting to her.

She now found herself walking down Mapledale in the same direction that the driver had gone. She wondered why she hadn't given him directions that would take him another route. He seemed harmless enough at first, but now she regretted being honest with him as to where Laurelwood Avenue was. Fortunately, she wasn't going quite that far. Besides, she rationalized, he'd probably be long gone by now.

Up ahead on her left, Shelby saw the tall stand of dense juniper hedges. She'd been afraid of passing this spot ever since she was about seven. It was here that she had come across a stray dog that had chased her the four blocks back to her house. It wasn't a big dog, more like a small beagle or a Jack Russell terrier, but it had nipped at her heels a few times before she reached the safety of home.

She instinctively always passed this spot at something of a run and decided to do so again. As she cleared the tall hedgerow, she could plainly see that the yard beyond it was empty. She breathed a sigh of relief and slowed down her pace.

With that, she felt a sudden and numbing pressure on the back of her head, saw a bright flash of light and went flying forward. In the confusion, she wondered what had hurt more, the back of her head or the side of her face where it had struck the sidewalk. Shelby rolled onto her back and felt herself slipping out of consciousness. Just before she did, she could see the figure of a man in a baseball cap silhouetted against the failing indigo of the brisk October evening.

The son of a bitch had hit her with his flashlight.

Chapter 2

Jack Sullivan was 32 years old. He stood just shy of six feet tall, had brown eyes and dark brown hair with a few sporadic grays. There was nothing extraordinary about his appearance. In truth, he was the kind of guy that could blend in easily with a crowd. What set him apart from everyone else was his unique line of work. Jack was something of a historian, but it was the subjects of his study that were quite different. He would research the histories and building dates of houses for architectural firms and real estate agents, but on occasion he would be hired by a paranormal research group to prove or debunk legends behind some of the most noteworthy haunted houses in America.

Furthermore, Jack had a keen talent for locating curious items, usually linked in some way to the occult or some famous legend. He would occupy much of his free time writing about these haunted houses and curious goods and had been published four times already. As far as the curious items went, some would wind up in his own collection while others were for clients that would pay him handsomely for his services.

It was one such client that had now sent him to New York City to act as purchasing agent for just such an item. Jack had located it only one week earlier. His client was ecstatic when Jack told him that it would be going up for auction. For a moment it looked as though Jack wouldn't be making his appointment. He'd been stricken just a few days earlier with a severe fever that had kept him in bed and unable to move. He was stubborn and refused to see his doctor about it. Visits like that seemed to him to be a waste of time and money. It was the flu and a doctor would simply prescribe Tylenol. As it was, after two days Jack was feeling much better and was well up to making the trip. Only a slight sniffle remained. It would take more than that to keep him from the job he loved.

Jack sat in the dimly lit room at Darby's Auction House in New York City surrounded by forty or so other people who had come to bid on the items presented. Some, it was clear, had come to purchase a specific item while others were just hoping to pick up on something of value for what they thought would be a song and a dance. One such man was Mr. Phelps: a short and pudgy balding man in his early sixties. It irritated Jack, and many others present, that he was driving up the cost of some items that he had no intention of purchasing. He was a true master. He knew just when to stop bidding so that he wouldn't be stuck with something that he really didn't want. Jack was now in such a bidding war against Mr. Phelps over the item he'd been hired to purchase.

As the auctioneer rattled off figures that ascended exponentially, Jack would raise his paddle at every other figure. The cost was now well over $2,000. He still had some leeway. His client had given him a price to stop bidding at and they were still nowhere near that amount.

"Do I hear three thousand?" the auctioneer asked. Mr. Phelps' paddle went up. "Three thousand... do I hear three thousand one?" Jack lifted his paddle into the air as he sniffled. The other people around him recoiled a bit with germaphobic disgust. "Three thousand one," the auctioneer continued. "Do we have three thousand two?"

No one raised their paddle, including the irritating Mr. Phelps. The auctioneer took a good look around the room before continuing.

"Three thousand one then... going once... twice... and sold to number 27 for three thousand, one hundred dollars."

Jack stood up and made his way past those around him that had been put off by the fact that he'd attended this auction and contaminated their sterile oxygen. He tucked his paddle into a binder and made his way over to an attendant that was standing beside the stage. The attendant handed him a form attached a clipboard and indicated where he needed to sign. After doing so, Jack was handed a carbon copy slip and much to the relief of many in the room, exited into the lobby.

Wiping sweat from his brow with a handkerchief and worrying that his fever was returning, Jack made his way over to a desk at the head of the lobby. For a moment he thought that he caught sight of a young woman staring at him through the large plate-glass windows from out on the street. As he glanced over, he noticed that there was no one there. Now he began to worry that he was starting to see things. He promptly approached the desk

13

and handed a cashier the carbon copy of the form he had just signed. The cashier rang up the amount and Jack withdrew a large stack of one hundred dollar bills from his wallet. He counted out thirty-one of them and handed the stack to the cashier, who likewise counted the stack and marked them with a disappearing ink. Jack signed one more form and was given yet another carbon copy slip. This he tucked into an inside jacket pocket, turned and exited the lobby onto the busy Manhattan street.

The sunlight was blinding. Reaching into his pocket and riffling past the form he'd just received, Jack withdrew his sunglasses and placed them on his face. His recent illness had left him slightly more sensitive to things than he had been in the past. He found that excessive light and noise were becoming more and more of an irritation. With a little luck, this would only be a temporary condition and he'd be right as rain in a few more days. Perhaps after returning to Cleveland and turning over his recent purchase, he'd take a few more days off, just to get himself a bit more set in the head.

Jack turned to his right and took a few paces before he noticed the young lady he'd thought he'd seen from the lobby standing before him with a stare of intent on her face. He looked her over once and saw that she was quite pretty. She was about the same age as he was, maybe a couple of years younger and a few inches shorter. She was quite slender, had straight shoulder-length light brown hair and the biggest, brightest blue eyes he had ever seen. Her skin was quite pale with a few light freckles on her nose and cheeks and, though she didn't seem to be wearing any makeup, her lips seemed to glisten with a light melon hue, much like the type that one would normally see on someone who was a redhead.

Beautiful as this woman was, something bothered him about her: like she was there to deliver a subpoena or give him some sort of bad news. Whatever it was, he didn't like it. He promptly turned around and walked the other direction. Something told him though that she was following. He quickly entered a taxi that was parked at the side of the road. He gave the driver the address of the hotel he was staying at and departed. As he looked out the window, he could see the woman still standing at the curb with a dejected look upon her face.

One hour later, Jack was sitting on the couch in his room at the Hotel Elysee on East 54th Street. He'd made the call to his client back in Cleveland while he was still in the cab, but only received an outgoing message from the cell phone he was calling. He left a message to call back and had been awaiting this call for nearly twenty minutes. He got up and made his way over to the liquor cabinet. No sooner had he placed his hand on the bottle of Jameson's Irish whiskey that his phone rang. It was a ring tone of two brief notes followed by a pause, made to emulate the way a telephone rings in Europe. Jack placed the bottle back in its original location and answered his phone.

"Are we happy?" asked a voice on the other end.

"We're very happy, Mr. Dresden," Jack replied. "Thirty one hundred and it'll be delivered to my place around three tomorrow afternoon."

There was a pause.

"Sully, you never cease to amaze me. What time is your flight due in?" Mr. Dresden asked.

"Should be in at Hopkins around eleven in the morning."

"Would you like me to send a car?"

"No thanks. I'll be alright," Jack said. "I'll just take a cab back to Lakewood."

"Are you sure? It's the least I can do."

"Really, It's no problem; especially with what you're paying me already."

"True. How are you feeling?"

"Still a little under the weather, but otherwise I'm alright. Just plan on being over around four tomorrow afternoon to pick up your purchase."

"Will do. You have a safe flight home and we'll talk tomorrow."

"Thanks. See you then."

Jack hung up the phone and placed it on the small end table next to the couch. It was getting late in the afternoon and Jack was now wondering what he was going to do about dinner. It'd have to be an early one, as he needed to be at LaGuardia by seven in the morning if he was going to make his flight back to Cleveland. Ever since the terrorist attacks in 2001, airlines had been asking that people arrive three hours early to go through screening. Jack knew well enough that screenings never took three hours, but with his luck, the one day he shows up later, he'd probably miss his flight.

Another headache was coming on. Jack walked back over to the liquor cabinet and this time was successful in pouring himself a short tumbler of whiskey… neat. He took a sip, swished it about in his mouth for a second and let the burn run down the back of his throat. He carried his glass over to the window and looked out across Central Park just a few blocks away. It intrigued him that there would ever be such a vast amount of green space in such an urban location. The closest he had back home was the Metroparks, and that was a good twenty minutes from the city. Sure, there was Edgewater Park, but he never really hung out there. Jack lost himself for a moment in the view below him and suddenly was drawn out of his trance by a sudden knock at the door. He turned around and stared across the room wondering who else, besides Mr. Dresden, could know that he was there.

He crossed the room and went to open the door but suddenly remembered that he wasn't back at home and that it could be anyone outside. He thought about it for a moment and looked through the peephole. Standing outside his room was the attractive woman he had seen on the street outside of Darby's earlier that day. With disbelief, he opened the door and walked over to the couch where he took a seat: his drink in his hand.

"Are you following me or something?" he asked without inviting the woman in.

"I guess, I am," she replied stepping across the threshold and looking about her. "You're Jack Sullivan, aren't you?" she asked as she closed the door behind her.

"Yeah, I'm Jack Sullivan. And *why* are you following me?"

"I read the article that Michael O'Malley had written on you in the Plain Dealer last Friday: '*Local Author, Historian Solves Riddle Of Man Missing For 60 Years*'."

"Oh, you read that?" Jack asked with a smile.

"Intriguing article. It must have been pretty hard to find him."

"Not really. All I did was look into his past and learned that he had once worked in Butte, Montana. I did some searches and found that he had left his family, gone back there to pursue an old flame, married her and died a few years later. Sure he used an assumed name when he did all of this, but he messed up by naming his son after his maternal grandfather. Anson is a particularly unusual first name; especially when coupled with a middle name like Portman. After I met with his children, they corroborated with the facts and that the dates and places pertaining to their father's life all matched up. I'll tell you this much, Anson P. 'Donaldson' wasn't very happy to learn that he was really the illegitimate son of a man from Cleveland, Ohio. He was interested to meet his half-brother though. Why is any of this of interest to you? Are you related to him as well?"

"No," the woman said shaking her head, "it's nothing like that."

"Okay, so, what is it then?"

"Well, I figured that if you could find a man that has been dead for over half a century, you might have some luck at finding one who's still alive…"

"An ex-boyfriend?" Jack interrupted.

"As well as a few young girls that *are* dead."

Jack paused for a second and stared at the woman. That was the last thing that he had expected her to say. He'd nearly spilled his drink. She went on.

"This was me." She handed Jack a leaflet with the headline: "*MISSING.*" Jack immediately looked at the picture of the young girl on the page and saw the resemblance at once. He read on to himself: his words almost inaudible.

"Missing: Shelby Louise Tomlinson. Age 14. Female. Five feet, five inches tall. Brown hair and blue eyes. One hundred and ten pounds. Missing since October 17th 1992. Last seen on Lynnwood Drive in Oakhurst, Ohio wearing blue jeans, brown boots, black tee shirt, white thermal shirt and blue denim jacket with colorful writing on it. Any information, please call Oakhurst Police at 216-…" Jack trailed off in his words and looked up at the now grown Shelby Tomlinson in astonishment.

"Fifteen years ago, I was abducted by a man while I was walking home from my friend's house. This man held me in what I think was a basement for fourteen days. There, I was assaulted… sexually… and quite frequently." Shelby paused for a moment as

17

though it would be quite difficult to go on. She continued nonetheless. "I don't remember all the details of what happened in the end, but the next thing I knew I was wandering about in the woods a few miles from my house. My clothes were bloody and I was covered in mud. It could have been that I was initially hit in the back of the head and had a concussion or that he'd kept me drugged. As near as anyone could figure, I must have fought him off and escaped. I couldn't remember anything like where I was or how long I had been walking... or even what he had looked like. But things are starting to come back to me... in dreams. Small details, like the sounds of a tractor and some sort of a chemical smell that reminded me of biology class. I don't know what it all means, but it must have something to do with what had happened to me."

"So why do you think this is all happening now?" Jack asked. He was intrigued.

"How well did you read the rest of that newspaper that your article was in?"

"Not thoroughly, I guess."

"You haven't opened your email lately, have you?"

"I've been sick"

"Had you opened it, you'd see what I'm talking about."

Jack walked over to his suitcase and pulled out his laptop. He brought it over to the couch where he had been sitting and booted it up. After a few moments of silence between him and his guest, he logged in to his email account and saw a number of unopened messages. A couple were from friends and associates but two were from an unknown user. One was marked "*PD Article*." He opened it up and saw the familiar article that he had just cut out and hung on his refrigerator the previous Friday.

"Yeah?" asked Jack.

"Read the article below yours."

Jack scrolled down to the headline written below the photograph and caption describing his work. The headline read: "*Rebecca Lowe, 12, Missing From North Coventry*." He continued to browse through the article for a few minutes before looking up at Shelby.

"She's been missing since last Wednesday night. You don't think she might be a runaway?"

18

"I'm telling you. It's the same guy. What's worse is that she's not the only one. I remember my abductor telling me that he was new to the area. I have a theory that he travels around and pulls this everywhere he goes."

"What makes you think that?"

"Open the other email," she instructed.

Jack closed the first email and opened the next one marked simply as "*Also Missing*."

It contained a series of articles. Each one had a similar headline about a girl, Caucasian, between the ages of eleven and fifteen, missing from some city and state. Three or four in a row would be from the same general location, but the last article from that location would be about a girl that was nearly abducted. All of these near abductions were the same story: a man claiming to be new to the area and asking for directions. All took place in the evening, as did the corresponding disappearances. Jack couldn't help but feel heartache at so many stories of missing girls.

"Well, you've done your research," Jack said as he closed the email and logged off. "What makes you so certain that this is the same guy?"

"It has to be him. I haven't thought about it in so long and now, last week, I start having dreams about it. Each time, there's just a little more. The morning after the first dream was when that article below yours was printed."

"You seem to be making good progress on this. Why do you need me?"

"Because there's something here that I'm missing," Shelby said with a touch of urgency. "I come across an article about an abducted girl from the area and it just happens to be printed below an article about a guy who finds missing people."

"Coincidence…" Jack began.

"I don't believe in coincidences. It has to be you that stops this guy. I'm certain of it."

"Haven't you gone to the police with all of this?

"They'd laugh at me; much like I'm sure you're doing right now."

Jack's voice now held a touch of concern, sympathy and honesty.

"I'm not laughing at you," he told her. "But why follow

me here to New York and not wait until I get back to Cleveland?"

"Rebecca Lowe can't wait. It's already been almost a week since she went missing. I managed to escape after fourteen days, so she may have… that long…"

"What do you think will happen after fourteen days?"

Shelby shot Jack a glance so horrible that words couldn't describe it.

"We're not thinking about that," she whispered, "and we're not letting it come to that."

Jack realized what this meant.

"My rate is usually two hundred dollars a day, plus expenses," he explained.

"That sounds reasonable."

Jack considered it for a moment.

"Look, I fly home in the morning and have an appointment at my place in the afternoon." He walked over to the small desk across the room and wrote down his address on a slip of paper. "Feel free to stop by in the evening and we can discuss how exactly we're going to go about this."

Shelby took the paper from him and started for the door. Suddenly a thought came to Jack.

"Hey, I'm about to go have dinner. Would you care to join me?"

Shelby looked at him curiously.

"No thank you. I'm not hungry."

"Very well. Have a safe trip home Mrs…" Jack hadn't noticed if she was wearing a wedding ring or not.

"It's Miss Tomlinson. I never married. But you can call me Shelby if you wish."

With that, Shelby Tomlinson closed the door behind her. Jack picked up his drink and returned to the window staring out at the city below. The streetlights were now coming on and he still needed to find a place for dinner. Seven o'clock came pretty early.

Chapter 3

The takeoff was as uneventful and completely forgettable as any that Jack could ever care to remember. It had been an early morning and he now looked forward to getting some rest on the flight back to Cleveland. They'd be up in the air for an hour and forty-five minutes and hopefully that would be enough time for Jack to catch up on some sleep. He'd been up for most of the night rehashing in his mind what had transpired earlier in the evening. True, he'd taken on unusual cases in the past, but this was the first time that he had taken even the slightest hand in an active missing person's case. He now began to wonder if he had just stepped out of his realm of expertise. Try as he might, he couldn't get the conversation with Shelby Tomlinson out of his mind. By helping her, he may have crossed a line with the police as well. He'd crossed it before and that had gotten him in considerable trouble.

A few years earlier, he had been driving on Interstate 90 when he noticed a long string of police cars approaching from behind. It was night and their flashing red and blue lights were noticeable from a considerable distance away. Jack soon realized that they were chasing after a car that was running at a high rate of speed with its headlights turned off. He started to pull to the shoulder, but at the last minute figured that he'd intervene and pulled back out in front of the rogue vehicle. The impact with the back of his Mazda was quite hard, but Jack was none the worse for wear. Besides, he had successfully stopped the fleeing driver before he could do any serious harm. As it turned out though, the police were anything but appreciative. Jack was slapped with a reckless operation citation and a separate ticket for interfering with official police business. The interfering charge was dropped, but the reckless operation ticket stuck. In the end, it cost Jack $150 plus court costs as well as another $485 for a new rear bumper. One thing he had learned was that it was sometimes better to stay out of it.

Every time he closed his eyes, Jack kept seeing the newspaper articles that Shelby had shown him the evening before. Try as he might, he couldn't shake the images from his mind. The events of the last twenty-four hours had seemed almost surreal, as though they were something from a dream. Had he really met with this woman last night or did he just stumble upon a story about an abducted girl from Oakhurst, Ohio and imagined the whole thing. Jack's head was hurting again and he realized that this was a crazy line of thought. His fever was coming back. What he needed at this point was a good shower and a long nap. The shower would have to wait. He closed his eyes and turned to his side trying to get in a few moments of sleep before landing. No sooner had he done this than the co-pilot chimed in over the speaker.

"Ladies and gentlemen, this is your co-pilot speaking. We are beginning our final approach into Cleveland. The weather is sunny and sixty-two degrees. The fasten seat belt sign will be lit momentarily and we ask that you remain in your seats until the aircraft has arrived at the gate. Please enjoy the rest of the flight."

Jack chuckled lightly as he remembered George Carlin's views on airline terminology, particularly the part where he talks about the term "final approach." The only other part from the skit that Jack could remember was Mr. Carlin saying something about people telling him to get on the plane. He'd say "I'm getting *in* the plane. Let Evel Knievel get *on* the plane." Jack began to laugh to himself quite heartily. Sitting up and buckling his seat belt, he noticed the lady across the isle glancing over with a distasteful look on her face. Jack didn't feel like explaining.

As he made his way up the concourse and toward the baggage claim area, Jack noticed a man in a chauffeur's uniform, complete with hat and driving gloves, holding a sign with the name "Jack Sullivan" written on it. Mr. Dresden had sent his driver after all.

The ride home was almost as uneventful as the flight had been. It was a pretty nice day, but Jack's eyes were still bothering him. He wore his sunglasses for most of the way, but after a time, he removed them.

"Rough night?" asked the driver.

"Not really," Jack replied. "Why do you ask?"

"The sunglasses. Looks like you been up partying most of the night."

"Oh. No. I've been sick lately."

22

"Well, I hope you're feeling better soon." There was a pause, as though the driver were trying to find something to make conversation about. "So what street you live on?"

"Hathaway. It's one block east of Bunts."

"Nice area."

Jack likewise thought for a moment of something to say. The driver seemed like a nice guy, somewhat bullish, but friendly nonetheless.

"So, have you worked for Mr. Dresden for very long?"

"A few months," the driver said. "Just moved back about a half a year ago."

"Oh. What did you do before this?"

"I was a merchant marine."

"No shit. So was I until a few years back. Sailed all over the Great Lakes. Who did you work for?"

"Uh… I was ocean. Worked mainly out of Louisiana."

"Ah."

A few minutes later, the driver dropped Jack off at his house on Hathaway Avenue in Lakewood, helped him with his bag and left him with the words that he'd be seeing him later that day when he and Mr. Dresden would return to pick up the package. Jack said goodbye and the driver pulled away.

Jack lived in a curiously arranged apartment on the third floor of a house. It originally served as the attic, but had been converted into living space some years earlier. The front entrance led up a set of stairs and to a pair of doors placed side by side. The first of these doors let to the second floor apartment, which was currently occupied by his landlord, a man named George. Jack had met George a few years earlier when he had worked as a deckhand on a Great Lakes freighter. George was a wheelsman then, but had since been promoted to first mate. The sailing season ran from mid-March until very early January and therefore, George was currently away on work.

The door next to George's opened directly to another set of stairs that let off right in the middle of Jack's living room on the third floor. It was a two-bedroom apartment, but Jack only used one of these. The other contained the many curious items that he had accumulated over the years. Jack kept the room padlocked and would never let anyone in there, let alone tell anyone what it contained. His friends had told him that the room would make for a good office, but he needed the space for storage. Therefore he kept his desk at the southern end of his living room.

Jack took his bag upstairs and upon opening the door was greeted by Fionn: his frantic and jubilant cat that was obviously very happy to see him. His other cat, Aislinn, was likely sitting in a window somewhere and could care less if he was there or not.

"Hello Stinky," he said as he scooped up the yellow cat with key lime eyes. "Miss me, did you?" He closed the door behind him and walked up the stairs into his living room where he set down his bag.

The cat rubbed his face affectionately across Jacks chin. Jack scratched his ears for a moment and set him down by his bag. He walked over to his kitchen table and began to leaf through the mail that had come over the last few days: a couple of bills and a bunch of advertisements. No sooner had Jack taken off his jacket than his phone began to ring. It was Corley, George's daughter that occupied the first floor apartment.

"Hey Corley," Jack said as he answered the phone.

"Hey, you home?"

"Just got in now. Thanks for bringing in the mail and looking after the cats."

"No problem. Hey, did you catch the Bruins game last night?"

"Missed it," replied Jack as he briefly thought again about his meeting with Shelby Tomlinson. "How did they do?"

"Beat the Fliers three to two in a shootout."

"That's great." Jack suddenly remembered the auction. "Oh, I need you to move your car out of the driveway in a bit. I have a package coming this afternoon and am going to keep it in the garage for an hour or two."

"No problem," replied Corley. "What is it, anyway?"

"Stick around and I'll show you. Or better yet, I'll have Mr. Dresden show you when he gets here. One thing's for sure, he always loves an audience."

"I have to run out for a while but should be back by two. I'll park on the street."

"Thanks again."

"Later," and with that word, Corley hung up.

Jack stretched out on his couch for a few minutes, turned on the television and watched the mid-day news. Afterward, he checked the rest of his email and answered some of his messages. There was nothing new from Shelby. He wondered when or if he would see her again. He'd given her his address and told her to stop by that evening, but she hadn't exactly given him a straight answer as to whether or not she would. On a whim, Jack thought that he'd look her up online, but could find no social network page or listed telephone number. Nonetheless, he decided to hook up his printer and print out the articles that she had sent to his email. There were more than he remembered there being the night before. After he'd finished with this, he was briefly tempted to do some research on another project he had been working on, but fought off the urge, logged out and turned off his laptop. He stretched back out on the couch and got a couple more hours of sleep.

Jack awoke to the sound of his doorbell ringing. He sat bolt upright and ran to the window. Parked outside was a white delivery van. Jack glanced over at the clock and saw that it was just after three in the afternoon. How long had the deliveryman been waiting outside for him? It's true that Jack wasn't a heavy sleeper but he could very well have kept him waiting for a good ten minutes. He quickly threw on his shoes, ran down the stairs to the front door and opened it just as the deliveryman was starting to walk back to his truck.

"Sorry about that," Jack apologized as he stepped out onto his porch.

"I'd almost given up on you," replied the deliveryman.

He handed Jack another form to sign, which he did at once. Jack chuckled as he did so, thinking that this item that he had picked up in New York was based on nothing but signatures and forms. He handed the clipboard back to the driver, who placed it on the passenger seat of his truck. Jack also thought this to be quite amusing. These trucks were equipped with passenger seats, yet never had he seen a passenger riding in one. The driver strolled around to the back of the truck and opened the door. There

25

sitting before him was a fairly sizable box measuring about five feet wide and three feet high. The deliveryman pulled down a two-wheeled dolly and Jack helped him to retrieve the package.

"So where do you want it?" he asked.

"Back here," Jack replied as he pointed up the driveway.

The two walked toward the back yard with the package. Jack ran slightly ahead and opened the broad door of the detached garage. He moved the charcoal grille to the side making room for the new package.

"Right here is good," Jack told him. The driver set the package down in the place indicated, pulled the dolly out from under it and without a word, walked back up the driveway. "Thanks," Jack added, but the reply was little more than a wave.

Corley stepped out through the side door, two beers in her hand, and approached Jack.

"So what is it?" she asked, brushing her red hair out of her face with her free hand.

"You'll see when Mr. Dresden gets here," Jack told her. "What do have there?"

"Great Lakes Nosferatu. I figured it might help out with the cold."

"Thanks." Jack took the beer, cracked it open using the bottle opener on his key chain and took a hearty pull. The brew was robust and hoppy, both qualities that Jack looked for in an ale. True it was no Guinness, his usual beverage, but it was nice to change things up from time to time.

As they sipped their beers, Jack told Corley about his trip to New York and all the things he got to see while there. He'd finally made it to the Statue of Liberty, something that he'd wanted to do his whole life and even found the time to make it back to Ellis Island. He decided not to tell Corley about his meeting with Shelby Tomlinson. He still wasn't even sure if he'd be taking on this case and thought it best to keep it to himself for the time being.

Just as they were finishing their craft beers, a red Cadillac DTS pulled into the driveway. Mr. Dresden and his chauffeur stepped out of the vehicle and approached the garage.

"So this is it then?" asked Mr. Dresden.

"It is," Jack replied. The chauffeur pulled out a razor knife and approached them. Corley took a nervous step back and watched as the wide, bullish man knelt down beside the box and set himself to the task of slicing up the cardboard package. The cardboard slowly gave way to reveal an old steamer trunk with the initials K.G. embossed on the lid. As the chauffeur put away the razor and stood up, Mr. Dresden took a step back and admired his recent purchase. He clasped Jack on the shoulder, who was smiling as well.

"You've done real good, Sully," Mr. Dresden congratulated.

"It's a trunk," Corley said, pointing out the obvious.

"It's not just any old trunk," corrected Mr. Dresden. "This trunk once belonged to Karl Germain, one of the greatest magicians of all time. And I can't wait to see what's inside."

Mr. Dresden crouched down and popped the two latches that had been keeping it shut for all these years.

"Moment of truth," he said as he produced an old and tarnished iron key from his pocket. He placed it in the keyhole at the front, gave it a twist and the lid released. "We have a winner!" he exclaimed. He lifted the lid slowly, peeked inside, let out a sigh and lifted the lid the rest of the way. The trunk was empty.

"I'm sorry Mr. Dresden," Jack said after a moment. "It certainly felt like it had contents in it."

"Sorry? What's there to be sorry about? After all these years it still works."

Jack and Corley both looked at him perplexed. Mr. Dresden closed the lid again and this time turned the key the opposite direction. They heard the cylinder click into the locked position. Mr. Dresden continued to turn the key until it clicked again. This was followed by an immediate thumping sound. Mr. Dresden smiled.

"Eureka!" he announced. "I give you the vanishing chest of Karl Germain!"

He opened the lid again and there before them sat a wide array of books, bottles, and other devices; their functions unknown.

"Incredible," whispered Jack as he crouched down beside the trunk.

"Karl Germain was full of surprises," Mr. Dresden explained with a smile on his face. "This will keep me busy for years." He stood up and reached into his pocket retrieving a checkbook and a pen and began to write out a check payable to John M. Sullivan. "I'm throwing an extra three thousand for a job well done. It's more than I could have hoped for."

Jack smiled, received the check and shook Mr. Dresden's hand with deep appreciation. Mr. Dresden and his chauffeur picked up the vanishing chest and placed it in the trunk of the Cadillac. There was no way that the hatch would close, so Jack pulled out some sash cord from the garage and tied the package in place. With another handshake, Mr. Dresden departed with his new acquisition. Jack returned to the garage, where he and Corley picked up and threw away the remnants of the shredded delivery box. She had offered him another beer, but Jack declined. He still wanted to take a shower.

Chapter 4

Jack stepped out of the shower, dried himself off and threw on his heavy terrycloth robe. He stood at the closet, next to his bathroom door, still unsure of what he was going to wear. It would be another cool October evening, so that probably meant a sweater and jeans. The question was which sweater to wear. If Shelby Tomlinson didn't show up by ten, he'd likely end up at McNamara's Public House on Lake Avenue for a few pints of Guinness. That would mean that he'd be outside with his friends quite a bit and should probably go with a turtleneck. On the other hand, if she did show up, he'd be inside his apartment with her for most of the evening and might not even make it up to Mac's. Suddenly, he heard someone in the living room clear their throat. Jack almost jumped out of his skin. He turned to see Shelby sitting on the couch, eying him curiously.

"I'm sorry," she apologized as she averted her eyes. "The door was unlocked and I let myself in. I'd have rung the doorbell, but there are three of them and none are marked."

"That's okay," replied Jack as he tightened up his robe. "I'll just be a moment."

He grabbed his dark green sweater from the closet and retreated into the privacy of his bedroom, where he closed the door and dressed himself. A couple of minutes later, he returned fully presentable.

Shelby was still sitting on the couch, but was now petting Aislinn. The gray and white cat slept calmly, purring beside Shelby as she caressed the back of her head.

"Be careful," he warned. "She bites."

"Seems harmless to me."

"Just letting you know." Jack picked up a pen and a binder from his desk across the room and took a seat in the chair beside Shelby. He opened up the binder, set the articles she had sent him on the coffee table and pulled out a notebook. "I want to start from the top with everything that you have so far." He quickly leafed through the articles, twenty-two in all, and jotted down the names and dates in something of a chronological order. Shelby's article, were it with these, would have made twenty-three. As soon as he had finished this, he looked up at her. "And you were the first?"

"As far as I know," she replied.

"October 17th 1992?"

"That's correct."

Jack added this to the top of the list.

"Have you tried to find out if there were any others before you?"

Shelby thought about it for a moment before replying.

"There were other abductions, but none of them seemed to be connected to me or the other girls who came afterward."

"What makes you say that?"

"Those cases were either solved, the age or ethnicity didn't fit, or there was too much time in between abductions."

"Hmm." Jack focused back on the chronology that he had written out. "I see here that there were four other girls missing from near Oakhurst in the months following your abduction. That doesn't seem to fit the pattern of this guy. One gets away and he moves on."

"I know, but like I said, I couldn't remember much about what had happened to me or anything about my abductor. He must have figured that he was safe."

"Seven months after your abduction, a girl named Lauren Call from Valleywood, nearly gets abducted by a man dressed in a business suit, driving a black Ford LTD."

"It was the same with me; only then he was posing as a pizza deliveryman."

"Have you ever made any attempt to contact Miss Call?"

"Yes, but her family had moved away shortly after she was attacked."

"And did you contact Valleywood High School to see where they forwarded the transcripts of her grades?"

"No. I didn't know that I could do that"

"Well," said Jack making a note in the margin of the notebook, "that's going to be one of my first stops. That leaves us with seventeen more girls in four more states. Thirteen of which are still missing and four of which escaped their abductor. Two of these missing girls are from around Pittsburgh. Five are from Flagstaff, Arizona, three from San Francisco, California and three more from all over Kansas. Pennsylvania is doable, but the others are somewhat of a haul. No easy task ahead of us."

"Let's focus then on the cases here around Cleveland. This is where he is right now and time's running out for Rebecca Lowe."

Jack quickly scribbled something in the margin of his notebook and looked up again at Shelby.

"Actually, I'm surprised that I haven't asked you this yet, but have any of the bodies of the missing girls ever been recovered?"

"No," replied Shelby quite matter-of-factly. "Any Jane Doe that has been recovered fitting the age, gender and race doesn't fit any of the missing girls from the area."

"So the question is, what's he doing with them?"

Shelby looked at Jack with horror.

"Besides the obvious." Jack felt bad for putting it like that. "If he's killing them in the end, what's he doing with the remains? Fifteen years of murder... someone is bound to find something."

"You'd be surprised. There are a lot of hiding places in this world."

"Well, I can start by trying to look up Miss Call. She may have married by now and may be going under a different name, but with some luck, there will be an alumni association at her school that I can contact. As far as the other cases go, I'm going to see if I can get a hold of the case files. That might prove to be a bit easier said than done. I'm sure the cases are still listed as open investigations and are not available to the public. Still, It wouldn't hurt to check."

"Mr. Sullivan, I greatly appreciate the effort that you're putting into this."

"Please, it's Jack."

"Well, thank you, Jack," Shelby said as she stood up.

"I have to tell you Shelby, I'm still not convinced that these cases are related to the disappearance of Rebecca Lowe. I mean, why would he come back here after all these years and start this all over again? Why not go on to another city like he's done in the past?"

"I don't know why. I just know that it's the same man."

"Well, I'll see what I can find. If you want to come over again tomorrow evening, I should have more by then."

With that, Shelby Tomlinson left Jack's apartment. He watched her from the upstairs window as she walked up the street and out of view.

Jack spent the next three hours thoroughly reading over all the articles that Shelby had lumped into the email marked *"Also Missing."* He found many connections between them but there were a few discrepancies. For starters, the vehicle was different from city to city. In Cleveland, it was a LTD, but in Pittsburgh it was a Lincoln Continental. In Arizona, he drove a Cadillac Deville. In San Francisco it was back to the Lincoln, but was a Town Car this time. In Kansas, it had been a Cadillac Escalade. Each time though, the vehicle in question was black. Whoever this person was, they obviously had money, or some connection to it.

Jack thought briefly on the stereotype that kidnappers typically drove around in white cargo vans. He knew this probably wasn't normally the case, but would make sense, as they don't have any windows in the back. The man they were now looking for must subdue his victims quickly. Jack remembered Shelby saying that she had been hit in the head and had probably received a concussion. Head wounds bleed pretty badly. Surely there would have been blood found somewhere indicating where these girls had been abducted.

As Jack read on, he found that his theory was correct. Quite a few of the articles mentioned blood being found in the area where these girls were last seen. Perhaps it was the case with all of them, but the other newspapers didn't feel the information was appropriate or relevant to the story. Jack began to wonder how long a person with a blow to the head would remain unconscious. It would have to be long enough for the kidnapper to get back to his house or place of safety where he was holding these girls. Jack just couldn't imagine this man having to stop on the way to render his victim unconscious again. That would have attracted too much attention.

Jack went to his bookshelf and pulled out a map of the greater Cleveland area. The first abduction, being Shelby back in 1992, took place on Lynnwood Drive in Oakhurst. Jack circled the area and marked it with a number one. The next abduction, the first in the stack, was Melanie Maguire. She was last seen with her friends on November 5th at Aberdeen Public Library in Aberdeen, Ohio. Jack found it on the map, just two cities away from Oakhurst, and began to circle that area as well but stopped himself. He was pretty sure that she wasn't abducted from the library. That would have been too public of a place. He must have gotten her while she was on her way home, like he had done with Shelby.

Jack read the rest of the article but saw no mention of blood discovered anywhere along her route home. He decided to boot up his laptop and go online. He searched records for a Maguire family in Aberdeen and was lucky to find only one listing from 1992. They lived nine blocks from the library. Jack circled the area on his map between the library and her house and marked it with the number two.

The next to vanish was Kellie Ripley of Cuyahoga Park. This article did mention blood discovered on Thermal Street near Broadway. Jack found it on his map, circled it and marked it with the number three. By this point, he was certain that the police had already done something like this, but perhaps he'd be able to find something that they had missed.

Number four was an eleven-year-old named Nadine Somerset. She was taken from Brunswick Street in Terrace Hill. She, like Shelby, had been at a friend's house, but this friend only lived a few doors away. Jack found the location on his map, circled it and marked it appropriately.

The next was Anne Perkins of Forestville. Like Melanie Maguire, she too had been abducted shortly after leaving the local library. Jack scanned the article and saw that Perry Memorial Library was just two blocks from her house. He found the library on his map, circled it and marked it with the number five.

The last case in the Cleveland area was that of fifteen-year-old Lauren Call. She had been attacked at around 8:30 in the evening of May 20th 1993 on Alameda Avenue near Westerly Boulevard in Valleywood. Apparently, her attacker had attempted to hit her in the head with a flashlight, but ended up catching her in the shoulder instead. She made it safely to a neighbor's house where the police were contacted.

According to the newspaper article, the man had attempted to lure her into his vehicle a few minutes earlier. When she had refused him and walked away, the man drove off but had hid his black Ford LTD somewhere nearby. He then hid himself between two parked cars near the end of a driveway and waited for her to walk past. When he had missed her head and she took off running, the man must have likewise run. She went on to describe the man as being in his early forties with thinning hair and a goatee. He was also wearing a black business suit.

Jack drew a circle around the area of Alameda and Westerly in Valleywood and marked it with the number six. He put down his pen and took a step back to get a better look at the map. The six marks definitely formed something of an arch around a general area, quite rural, but Jack knew that it couldn't possibly be that easy. He was also certain that the police had looked into this as well. Perhaps the abductor had meant to leave a pattern like this and that it was intentionally deceptive. Nevertheless, he figured that he'd take a look into real estate transactions that took place in that area between May of 1993 and March of 1995; the date that the first abduction took place in Pittsburgh. He had a few friends that worked for different real estate agencies and was certain that it'd be no trouble for them to look up this info. In the meantime, he'd make a visit to Valleywood High school to see what they had on Lauren Call. Perhaps they could tell him more than the newspaper had written.

Jack looked at the clock and saw that it was well after midnight. There was no point in heading up to McNamara's at this hour. Most of his friends would be gone by now. He closed up his binder, turned off his laptop and walked over to the couch where he turned on the television and fell asleep watching a ghost hunting show on a cable network.

Chapter 5

Jack awoke early the following morning. He caught the lead stories on the news, shaved and took a shower. After throwing on some clothes, he headed up to the gas station around the corner from his house and bought a twenty-ounce cup of coffee with five hazelnut creamer. Afterward, he stopped by his friend Maxine Rybarczyk's office near the corner of Detroit and Warren Road.

Maxine was a fairly successful real estate agent in the area. Many times in the past, she had hired Jack to look up property information on houses that she was listing. The things that he would come up with were phenomenal and much more than anyone could have hoped for. Not only could he tell her things such as dates of construction and additions, as well as building costs, but he could also give the names of people who lived in these houses, their occupations, how many children they had, what year the plumbing was installed and how many people had been born and died in that house. Much of this, Maxine wouldn't include in the property description, but it was always nice to have it on hand, should the prospective buyer be interested to know. It helped that, on top of everything else, Jack was also an accomplished genealogist.

As Jack entered Maxine's office, he could hear that she was currently with a client. There was much laughing coming out of her back room and he knew that she had just closed a deal. She had a great personality that always made people feel comfortable when dealing with her. As the door closed behind Jack, it made a chiming sound that told Maxine that she had another customer. She excused herself briefly from her clients to greet her new arrival.

"I'll be with you in a…" she began, but saw that it was Jack. "Ah, Jack, I'm glad you're here. I want you to meet Mr. and Mrs. Kowalski."

Jack followed her into the back room where a younger couple was seated before her desk. They stood up to greet him as he entered.

"Jack, I'd like to introduce you to Tom and Nancy

Kowalski. Tom and Nancy, this is Jack Sullivan" Maxine announced as the three of them shook hands. "Tom and Nancy have just purchased the old Norman mansion."

"I see," said Jack in astonishment. He knew that Maxine had been trying to sell that property for well over a year, but had never received any serious offers.

"Jack's the man that did the research on that house."

"Is that so?" asked Tom Kowalski with piqued interest.

"So tell me Jack," continued Nancy, "Maxine says that it's absolutely false that Mr. Norman butchered his neighbors. Is that true?"

"It's true." Jack declared. "The only thing that Mr. Norman is guilty of butchering is the occasional chicken for dinner. Though what has been left out of the legend is that his second wife gave birth to their first child just six months after they were married, which would have been eight months after his first wife passed away. You do the math."

"That's really something," Tom marveled. "Have you done much more research on that house?"

"Some, but I'm sure there's a lot more to be found. There always is."

"Wait a second," Nancy said with a hint of realization in her voice, "Are you the same J. M. Sullivan that wrote the book on Maul Manor?"

"Yeah, that's me," said Jack. "Wrote that one with my friend Mark Schmidt. I also wrote Lake Erie Ghosts Ships, Haunted Lorain County and a book called Ohio's Dangerous Curiosities, which was about a bunch of supposed cursed items from around the buckeye state."

"We really liked 'Maul Manor: Fact and Fiction'," Tom told him. "Would you be interested in writing about the Norman mansion in the future?"

"Perhaps. I'm a little tied up for the moment, but once time allows, I'm sure that I'll be writing about area legends again."

"Well, don't hesitate to call us if you do," said Tom. "We'd be more than happy to help you in any way that we can."

"Thanks," Jack replied.

"So what brings you by today, Jack?" Maxine asked.

"Um… It can wait until later."

"Oh, that's okay," Tom said. "We were just on our way out. We'll see you later, Maxine?"

"I'll drop the keys off this afternoon."

"We'll see you then," Nancy said as they left the office. "And it was nice meeting you, Jack."

Jack waved as the door closed behind the couple with a chime.

"So what can I do for you Jack?" Maxine asked as she took a seat behind her desk and organized some papers. Jack likewise took a seat and pulled out his binder.

"I'm going to need some help."

After leaving Maxine's, Jack made a stop at the bank to deposit the check that Mr. Dresden had written him the previous afternoon. He was now on his way out to Valleywood. As he drove south on Interstate 77, he thought about what he had just told Maxine nearly a half an hour earlier. She certainly didn't approve of him getting involved in a police investigation, let alone one that might have involved murder. She agreed when he mentioned his thoughts about this case being beyond his realm of expertise.

"You should stick with haunted houses and cursed items," she had told him. "I'd hate to see you get wrapped up in something that puts you in over your head."

Despite all that, she agreed that she would take a look into any real estate transactions that had taken place for that location between the dates he had mentioned.

"I don't know what good it'll do you though," she'd said. "There are a lot of rental properties in that area and it's likely that the man you're looking for lived in one of those. There would be no record of his lease with the county either."

Still it was worth a shot. Besides, Jack didn't think that the man was a renter. It'd be too risky to keep a person hidden in a rental house. After all, a landlord could stop over at any time. Jack had asked her to start with houses that were more isolated, where screams wouldn't be noticed by neighbors: perhaps near a wooded area or a creek bed. Remembering what Shelby had told him, Jack found it hard to believe that a fourteen-year-old girl would be able to run down a suburban street, covered in blood, without attracting attention: even at night. It was more likely that she had run from her captor through woods or a ravine the entire way. He'd also remembered her mentioning that she'd heard something like a tractor. This would indicate a rural area.

Jack pulled into the parking lot of Valleywood High School, entered the building and made his way directly to the principal's office. He approached the secretary's desk and introduced himself.

"Good morning. My name is John Sullivan. I have an appointment with your assistant principal, Mr. Haas."

Jack could hear some commotion coming from an office just beyond the secretary's desk.

"You'll have to take a seat and wait until you're called upon Mr. Sullivan," the secretary informed him. "I'm afraid that we're quite busy at the moment."

With that, Jack thanked her and sat down on a bench a few feet away from a sixteen-year-old boy with a shaved head. By the scowl on his face, he could tell that this boy was in some sort of trouble and remembered, almost fondly, the trouble that he and his friends used to get into when they were in high school. One time they had gotten busted for lighting paper airplanes on fire and throwing them from the second floor window of the science lab. He remembered that their assistant principal wasn't very impressed. That little stunt had earned them all a two-day suspension.

The door to Mr. Haas' office opened and a boy exited looking quite put out.

"Mr. Nash!" the assistant principal announced, "you're next!" As the two boys passed each other, they both cracked something of a grin. "And get that damned smile off your face!"

The second boy continued on to the office wearing his scowl once again. The door slammed shut and Mr. Haas began berating him. Jack felt bad that he had caught this man on what seemed to him to be a bad day. From the brief glimpse that he had caught of Mr. Haas, he seemed like the type of man that you didn't want to cross. He was stocky with big hands and had what seemed to be a bright red face, but that might have been because he was furious at the moment. He reminded Jack of a gym teacher he'd once had in middle school: the kind of guy that would throw you across the locker room if you smarted off to him.

After a few minutes, Jack began to wonder if maybe he should come back on a better day. A moment later, the door to the assistant principal's office opened and the boy with the shaved head exited. As he passed Jack, he eyed him with a curious glance as though he too were in trouble. Mr. Haas followed the boy out and made one more comment to him.

"We'll see you next week."

Jack easily figured out that the boys had just been suspended. He couldn't help but wonder if they had been caught throwing lit paper airplanes from the science lab window.

"Mr. Sullivan," the assistant principal said in a calmer voice standing over him, "I must apologize for the wait. You wouldn't believe some of the shit these kids think they can get away with these days." Jack actually could, but thought better of telling him this. "Please, follow me to my office."

Jack did as he was instructed, only this time, Mr. Haas left the door open and there was no shouting.

"So I understand, Mr. Sullivan, that you're attempting to locate one of our former students?"

"That's correct," Jack replied. "Her name is Lauren Call. She transferred from here just after the 92 - 93 school year."

"Lauren Call... I remember her. She was that girl that was nearly kidnapped that spring. Left here because of all the negative attention that she was getting at school, I think. I had just started that year and was coaching the wrestling team." Jack knew this man had worked in phys-ed at some point. "Why are you trying to find out about her?"

"I'm currently working a missing persons case and believe that the two may be connected." Jack saw no harm in telling him that much.

"Is it that Lowe girl that's gone missing?"

"I'm afraid I'm not at liberty to give that information out."

"You a cop?"

"No."

"A private dick?"

"No. I'm a historian."

"A historian?" Mr. Haas glared at him with a confused look on his face. "What's a historian doing working a missing persons case?"

"Honestly, I've been asking myself that same question for the last couple of days."

"So what can we do to help?"

"Well, I'd simply like to know what school she transferred to after she left here."

Mr. Haas looked at his watch and compared it to the time that was displayed on the clock on the wall. He looked out the window for a moment and back at Jack.

"Okay, follow me."

Mr. Haas pulled a set of keys out of his desk drawer, stood up and exited the office with jack following closely behind him. They entered the empty hallway and walked over to a door. The word "*Records*" was engraved into a plaque just above the door frame. Mr. Haas unlocked the door, reached in and turned on the lights. The two men entered.

"This is where we keep every account of every student that has ever passed through these doors. Everything is alphabetically arranged. You're looking for Call. That's C-A-L-L?"

"That's correct," Jack replied.

Mr. Haas approached a tall filing cabinet, opened it and started to leaf through the files, reading quietly the names written at the top of each.

"Cain Mitchell, Cain Stephen, Cairn Brittany, Calder Martin, Caldwell Carla, Caldwell David, Call James... here we are, Lauren Call." He pulled the file, opened it up and flipped through a few pages. He found one and read the file quietly to himself. For a few moments, Jack thought that either there was nothing mentioned in the file or that Mr. Haas wasn't going to tell him. Suddenly, the assistant principal slammed the file shut, put it back in its place and closed the drawer.

"Wellington," he said turning to Jack. "She moved to Wellington."

Jack pulled out his notebook and pen and jotted down a quick note.

"Wellington's not that bad," Jack said as he closed his notebook. "That's just in Lorain County."

"I'm afraid that's all I can tell you."

"Thank you very much, Mr. Haas. You've been extremely

helpful."

The two men exited the records room and Mr. Haas escorted Jack to the front entrance of the school.

"Well, I wish you luck Mr. Sullivan."

"Thank you," Jack said as he extended his hand. Mr. Haas firmly grabbed it, shook it and laughed a little. "What's so funny?" Jack asked, slightly amused.

"Historians solving missing persons cases. What's next? Math teachers fighting fires?"

As Mr. Haas walked away, Jack began to see the humor in all of this.

It was now mid-day and Jack was feeling a bit hungry. He pulled into the back parking lot of the Cravings Café on Lake Road in Rocky River, grabbed his laptop and notebook and walked inside. He ordered a large mocha and an apple cinnamon muffin and took a seat on a brown leather couch at a coffee table where he set his beverage, food and laptop down. He took a sip from the mocha, wiped the cream from his upper lip and booted up his computer.

Finding Lauren Call proved to be much easier than he had first thought it would be, especially with nearly everybody now using social networking sites. All he did was log into his home page and look up Lauren Call in the Wellington class of 1996. There she was: Lauren Call-Ferris. She had married after all. Fortunately, her page was listed as "viewable by everyone", which made the task much easier. Jack saw among her listed friends, a man named Robert Ferris. There were a number of postings on her page from this man: some quite romantic. Obviously, Robert was Lauren's husband. Jack made a few notes and closed his social networking page. He then ran an internet search on Robert Ferris, Wellington, Ohio and hit enter. It brought up a listing on Rowell Road. Jack wrote down the address and phone number, turned off his computer and quickly finished his mocha and cinnamon muffin. He packed up his laptop and notebook and walked out to his car where he pulled out his phone.

Conversations like this, he thought, were always better held in private. He never liked the idea of someone overhearing what he was discussing. He'd felt nervous enough about talking with

Mr. Haas back at Valleywood High School with the door to his office opened.

Jack dialed the number he'd found online, double checked it and hit *send*. The voice that answered after a few rings was that of a woman.

"Hello?" the lady answered.

"Yes, Hello," Jack said immediately. "My name is Jack Sullivan and I was wondering if you could help me. I'm trying to locate a Lauren Ferris that graduated from Wellington High School back in 96. She would have been Lauren Call back then."

"Yes," the woman replied, "that's our daughter-in-law. To what is this matter concerning?"

"Well, Mrs. Ferris, I'm afraid that this is something of a sensitive matter and would feel more comfortable discussing it only with Lauren."

"You're going to have to tell me what it is, otherwise I won't put you in contact with her."

"Very well, I'm currently working a missing persons case and believe that she may be of some assistance."

There was a long pause on the other end. For a moment, Jack thought that she had hung up and that it'd be back to square one. Suddenly, Mrs. Ferris spoke up.

"Lauren hasn't spoken of that in many years now. The only time that I had ever heard about it was shortly after she had gotten engaged to our Robbie. She said that it was the most horrifying thing that had ever happened to her."

"Mrs. Ferris, I really need to speak with her."

"I seriously doubt that she'll want to talk about it."

"I'm just hoping that she can give me a little more information than was in the papers. With some luck they'll be able to catch this guy and lock him up for good."

There was another pause.

"I'll pass along your phone number to her, but I can't guarantee that she'll call."

"That's okay. I really appreciate it."

Jack waited for her to get a pen and paper. When she came back, he gave her his phone number and the two hung up. The ball was now in her court.

Chapter 6

Jack arrived at his apartment ten minutes later. No sooner had he reached the top of his stairs, that his phone began to ring. The number that came up was a 440 area code: Lorain County. Jack scrambled to get out his pen and notebook as he answered the phone.

"Hello?" he said into the phone. There was no reply. He was about to repeat himself when a soft voice came over the line, almost in a whisper.

"Are you close to catching him?"

Jack paused. He didn't know quite what to say.

"I'm not sure. Is this Lauren?"

"Yes. I got your message and was debating whether or not to call. You must understand, that part of my life is long behind me now and I've moved on from it as best I could."

"I understand. I'll make this as quick as possible for you."

"Does this have to do with that girl that's missing from North Coventry?"

Jack thought for a moment and realized that it would be wise to be honest with her on this part.

"Yes, it does," he replied.

"I've been following it on the news. But why do you think this is the same person? North Coventry is miles from Valleywood."

"There are a few similarities in the case."

Jack figured that it would be best to keep his client anonymous and make no mention of her. Furthermore, he decided against telling Lauren about the other cases in the other states. That might upset her and the conversation could be over just like that.

"I see that the girl does look a lot like some of the others that had gone missing, but why did he wait so long in striking again?"

"I don't know," Jack lied.

"The only other thing that I can see as being similar is the blood that was found on the sidewalk. They found that at the scenes where some of the other girls had gone missing too, right?"

Jack hadn't come across that information anywhere in the article on Rebecca Lowe.

"Where did you read that?" he asked.

"I didn't read it. It was mentioned in a newscast last week. You haven't been watching the news?"

"I've been sick lately and must have missed it." Jack didn't want to tell her that he'd only been hired onto this job a couple of days earlier or that he had been in New York City. That seemed irrelevant. "Look," he continued, "is there anything else that you can remember from the night that you were attacked?"

"Nothing more than I told the police. He drove a black Ford LTD that smelled like cigarettes, was balding and had a goatee. There was also some acrid chemical smell on him."

"A chemical smell?" Jack had heard this before from Shelby, but it wasn't mentioned in the article about Lauren.

"Yeah, it was really bitter and putrid. Made me feel sick."

"And you smelled this when you were talking to him?"

"Yes. That was one of the reasons I had stopped talking to him. It was right afterward that he started acting all creepy."

"Can you describe the flashlight that he hit you with?"

"Not really. He hit me from behind so I didn't get a look at it, but it felt quite heavy, like something a cop or a security guard or a night watchman would carry."

"How did you know it was a flashlight?"

"He shined one in my face just before he hit me. What else could it have been?"

"How badly was your shoulder hurt? Did you need to go to the hospital?"

"My shoulder wasn't hurt at all. He hit me in the back. And yes, I had to go to the hospital. I had two broken ribs."

Jack thought about this inaccuracy for a few moments before continuing with his questions.

"According to the article that I read, you were attacked on Alameda near Westerly. Were you on your way home?"

"I wasn't attacked on Alameda, I was attacked on *Westerly* near Alameda, and no, I wasn't on my way home. I was sneaking out to see my boyfriend, Sean."

Jack quickly jotted this down.

"I'm assuming that the police questioned your boyfriend."

"Of course. It was really quite embarrassing too. We broke up right after that."

"And what was Sean's last name?"

"No… I'd rather you didn't talk to him about this. The police had put him through enough."

"Very well," Jack continued, "back to the attacker. Was there anything interesting about his voice or the way in which he spoke: as though he wasn't from the area?"

"He said he was new to the area but, do you mean like an accent or something?"

"Yeah, like an accent or something funny about the way he said a certain word?"

Jack was also something of an expert on geographical dialects and vernacular.

"I'm afraid not. He sounded just like anyone else you'd meet. But I do know this: if I ever heard his voice again, I'd certainly recognize it."

"Why do you say that?"

"It's not something that you easily forget. That night's going to be etched into my memory for the rest of my life. I may have gotten over it and put it behind me, but I'll never forget it. Was there anything else that you wanted to ask?"

"Just one more question. Was there anything peculiar about the business suit that he was wearing, like a pin or anything?"

"Mr. Sullivan," Lauren said with a touch of confusion, "he wasn't wearing a business suit." Jack listened very closely to what she said next. "He was wearing a chauffeur's uniform."

Jack paused for a moment, thought really hard on her words and wrote them down.

"Lauren, thank you for taking the time to talk to me about this."

"Good luck in finding him Mr. Sullivan, but be careful. He doesn't seem the type to go down without a fight."

With that, Lauren Call-Ferris hung up the phone.

Jack took a seat at the desk across his living room, flipped open his laptop and turned it on; just in case he would get struck with an idea and wanted to look it up before the thought escaped him. He pulled the articles that Shelby had sent him out from his binder and set the stack next to his laptop. He started flipping through them until he came to the article on Lauren Call. He found the part of the story that mentioned her attacker as wearing a business suit and amended it so that it read *chauffeur's uniform.* He scanned over the rest of the article and found the other inaccuracies. He wrote down the words *Westerly near Alameda* and *struck in the back, not the neck... two broken ribs... hospitalized.* He found two other typos as he read on. For starters, the article said five missing, not four. Also, the word Ford was misspelled as *Frod.* These he also amended. He shuddered to think that the writer of this article might still be working in the newspaper industry.

Jack sat back in his chair and reviewed everything that he had in his notebook. He was convinced. The cases were in fact connected. It was Lauren telling him of the blood found on the ground at the scene where Rebecca Lowe had gone missing that made him realize this. It wasn't that he had any reason to doubt Shelby, but Jack was the type of person that had to see it for himself, or get it from a second source, before he would believe most things. Had there been a mention of blood found on the sidewalk in the Rebecca Lowe article that Shelby had given him, he would have seen the connection from the start.

It was getting towards mid-afternoon and Jack still had much to do. He'd have to hurry if he was going to make it to the Cuyahoga County Sheriff's Headquarters before their offices closed for the day.

The main front office at the sheriff's headquarters was noisy and full of people busy milling about: some carrying paperwork with them and others answering phones. Upon his arrival, Jack had spoken with a receptionist and had made a request to view some files. The receptionist gave him a form to fill out with the names and dates of the cases. After he had done so, she took the form, told him to have a seat and that someone would be with him shortly.

Nearly a half an hour had passed and Jack was getting worried. He knew that the offices would be closing at five and that he wouldn't have enough time to view all of the files thoroughly.

This would mean making more than one trip down here and he absolutely hated multiple visits for the same reason. It got old for him as well as the people that he'd have to deal with. After a few more minutes, a deputy stepped out through a door beside the counter.

"John Sullivan?" the deputy asked. Jack stood up.

"I'm here," he replied, lifting his hand as though he were back in high school and attendance was being taken.

"If you'll follow me…"

Jack trailed the deputy through the door and followed him to a cubicle where he was instructed to take a seat. Jack obeyed.

"I see here," the deputy began as he looked over a form attached to a clipboard, "that you wish to view files 19921105MAGM, 19930106RIPK, 19930202SOMN and 19930317PERA… well, you can't."

"I can't?" Jack was surprised with his bluntness.

"No, you can't," the deputy repeated. "These are still part of an active investigation and we don't release the information in these files until the case is closed or it becomes listed as inactive, which usually takes place twenty years after the files have been opened. Now," said the deputy placing the clipboard down on his desk, "I need to ask why you want to see these files."

"Okay," began Jack, "I'm looking into the disappearance of Rebecca Lowe and believe that these files may be connected to her."

"And what makes you think they're connected?"

"Have you read those files?"

"Have you?"

"No," said Jack indignantly, "but I've read newspaper articles related to those cases and I think there's going to be much more in the files."

"There's always more in the files. Newspapers only print the basic facts: that and what we release to them."

"So you're telling me that there are certain things that were intentionally kept from the public."

"Yes, Mr. Sullivan, there are certain things that we prefer to keep to ourselves in case a tipster comes forward with information that we've kept from the media. This is how we verify the legitimacy of a tip. Aside from that, there are details about each case that are a little too gruesome to be printed."

"I see."

"No, I don't think you do. The last thing that we need right now is some private investigator coming in here and trying to do the job that we were hired to do. I want you to stop looking into this."

"What harm could an extra set of eyes do?" Jack asked with a hint of astonishment.

"More than you could imagine. I shouldn't be telling you this, but we do have a person of interest in the Rebecca Lowe case. I'm not saying that it's a prime suspect or anything, but we don't want to scare him off. Now, what I want you to do is to go home and hang up this case. Forget that you ever got involved in it."

Jack thought for a moment about what this meant. He'd reached the end of his case. He hated putting an effort into something and then walking away from it, but it looked as though his hands were tied.

"Very well," Jack told him. "Just do me a favor and take a look at those files. You may find something that someone missed back then."

Jack stood up and began to leave the cubicle when the deputy stopped him.

"Look, I don't know who hired you to this case, but here's my card. If that person has any questions, I'd be more than happy to answer them."

Jack took the card and looked at it.

"Sheriff's Deputy Edward John Lauber," he read. "Thanks. I'll pass it along."

Chapter 7

Jack sat at the desk in the living room of his apartment with his laptop open before him. To his left sat three books opened to various pages. He had multiple windows open on his screen and kept clicking between them. A black notebook sat just to his right where he occasionally jotted down little notes. Just beyond the notebook sat a cold bottle of Great Lakes Edmund Fitzgerald Porter. He set his pen down, picked up the beer and took a swig. He set it back down and glared at the computer screen. A moment later, there was a knock at the door below.

"It's open," he told the visitor.

He heard the door open and close. Light footsteps carried Shelby Tomlinson up the stairs and into his living room. She came around the banister and pulled up a stool beside Jack's desk. She looked over the books that he had open before him and what was on the screen. None of it looked like it had anything to do with Rebecca Lowe or any of the other missing girl's cases.

"What's all of this?" she asked, a touch of agitation in her voice.

"It's about a possessed rag doll from Iowa that I've been trying to track down." Jack said, still glaring at the screen. "I think I may have found a lead to its whereabouts."

"And this is related to my case how?"

"It's not."

"Jack, I had hoped that you'd take this case a bit more seriously than…"

"I take it very seriously," Jack interrupted as he turned to face her. "Look. I spoke with Lauren Call earlier today."

"You found her?"

"Yeah, it wasn't that hard. Anyway, she told me her side of the story. There were a few discrepancies between what she told me and what was printed in that newspaper article."

"Such as?"

"Well, for starters, she wasn't hit in the shoulder, she was hit in the back. Also, the location of her attack was slightly off."

"What else?"

"Her attacker wasn't wearing a business suit. He was

dressed as a chauffeur."

"A chauffeur? Really?"

"That's what she told me."

"Then what?"

"Then nothing. I thanked her for talking to me about it, we said goodbye and hung up. One other thing…"

"What's that?"

"Apparently, there was blood found on the sidewalk close to where Rebecca Lowe went missing."

"So…"

"So I have absolutely no doubt that her disappearance is connected to you and the other girls."

"It's about time you got it. So why aren't you trying to find out more right now?" she asked him, a puzzled look on her face.

"Because after I got off the phone with Lauren Call, I went to the Cuyahoga County Sheriff's Department to view the files on the other missing girls and was told to drop the case."

"Why?"

"Because they say they have a 'person of interest' and don't want me scaring him off."

"Did they say who it was?"

"No. They're not going to divulge something like that to me. But if they're close to catching him, then there really is no point in me continuing this investigation. We should just let them do their job."

Shelby's head hung low. She couldn't believe what she was hearing.

"And I was so certain that you'd be the one to solve this."

"Well, it won't be me, it'll be the authorities. Also, there's no charge for the work I've already done. I didn't give you any results."

"I don't care about that."

"Look, Shelby, this is the reason that we have police and sheriff's departments. They're the ones who go after people like this, not historians. I'd love to help you, but there really isn't any more that I can do."

"Sure there is," she said as she raised her head. Jack could see that there were tears welling up in her eyes. "You don't have to actively pursue the kidnapper, just find out more about the other

50

cases; for me. I'm telling you that the key to finding him is in the cases of these other girls. Find what you can and turn it over to the police or whoever you like."

"But they think they already have their man."

"And if they catch him, all he'll get convicted with is abducting Rebecca Lowe. What about the other girls that he abducted? What about me? Anything that you find can be given to the authorities to link him to the other disappearances."

"Of course there's that."

"Also, they could have the wrong guy. If anyone can find this out, you can."

"What makes you say that?"

"From what I've seen so far, you use some pretty unorthodox methods when it comes to locating information. Methods that the police won't use."

Jack took a long, hard look at Shelby. He considered what she had just said very carefully.

"If I continue this, it's just going to be the girls that were abducted immediately after you were. No more Rebecca Lowe. If I find a correlation between them, I'll hang on to it, but set it to the side. If I find out who it is, beyond even the slightest doubt, I hand everything over to the proper authorities. Are we agreed?"

Shelby dried her eyes and smiled.

"Agreed."

"Alright then, here's the rest of what I found out. Whoever this man is, he has money, or at least some connection to it. In every near abduction case, he was driving a luxury car of some sort. He uses a blunt object to subdue his victims: preferably a large flashlight. There's some sort of chemical smell that accompanies him along with the smell of cigarettes. When you escaped from him, you were found in the woods. My guess is that he lived very close to those woods."

"So we're looking for a rich chemist that smokes, lives near woods and carries a flashlight?"

"Something like that," Jack replied with a smug grin on his face.

"What about the uniforms that he wore?"

"Could have been picked up from any thrift store."

"So... a thrifty rich chemist?"

"I'm just saying."

"This isn't getting us anywhere, Jack."

"We have to look at the bigger picture here. These things might all be related to the kidnapper's line of work. Who uses a big flashlight?"

"Someone who works at night," she declared.

"Okay, that's a start. Who works at night?"

"I don't know, a night watchman?"

"That's a good thought. We'll remember that."

"What about the cigarette smell?"

"Coincidental," Jack pointed out. "Anyone can smoke."

"But the car smelled of it."

"So, the person doesn't empty their ashtray very often. How about the luxury car... Who drives that?"

"Rich people, old people, car dealers, chauffeurs... Hey!"

"There!" Jack said with astonishment. "That's another thought, but I doubt this guy would remain in his work uniform if he was trying to kidnap someone. It's worth keeping in mind though."

"What about the chemical smell?"

Jack took a deep breath, held it for a second as he thought and puffed it out.

"Got me."

There was a long pause between them. They exchanged a quick smile that was followed by a few more moments of awkward silence. Jack was about to say something, but Shelby beat him to the punch.

"Jack, I've got to get going. Can we meet up again tomorrow evening?"

"Sure. Actually, I was about to head out myself for a drink. I was wondering if you'd like to join me."

"Thanks for the offer, but I'm going to have to pass."

"I see. Well then, I'll catch you tomorrow night."

With that, they both stood up and Jack walked Shelby to the stairs.

"Be safe going home," He told her.

"Thanks, I will."

Shelby descended the stairs and exited through the door below. As she left, Jack thought to himself that she still looked attractive, even as she was walking away.

McNamara's Public House was unusually packed for a Thursday night. Jack had some difficulty in finding a decent parking spot. As it was, he had to walk nearly a block to get to the place. At least the spot that he found was well lit.

As he entered the establishment, he could see why there was such a crowd. At the front of the room, placed right in front of the dartboard, was a four-piece Irish band called Mary's Lane. At first, Jack had thought that the jukebox was turned up, but as soon as he stepped to the door, he could see that he was wrong. As he took off his distressed leather jacket and hung it on the back of a stool, he caught the attention of Positive Bill, a long-time friend of his, who happened to also be the bartender. Bill's nickname had come from the old school slang; where a fat guy was called Slim and a bald guy was dubbed Curly. Bill was something of a cynic: thus the play on his name. Without a word, Positive Bill picked up a Guinness glass and pointed to it.

"Awe, would ya?" Jack asked in an odd sort of mumble. It had been part of a running joke that had been going on for a few months now. Lately, the guys at McNamara's had been talking like Ted Levine's character Buffalo Bill in *The Silence of the Lambs*.

Bill chuckled as he pulled down on the Guinness handle, filling the glass three quarters of the way full. He left it under the tap to let it settle and came over to greet Jack.

"How you doing tonight?" he asked.

"Not too bad," Jack replied as he extended his hand. Bill shook it. "You?"

"Can't complain. We got a pretty good crowd in here tonight. How was New York?"

"It was good. I finally got to see the Statue of Liberty."

"Did you go up?"

"Yeah, but only up to the crown. The torch is still closed."

"Oh, hang on," Bill told him as he walked back over to the Guinness handle and completed the pour. He returned with Jack's beer, walked over to the cash register and touched the screen a few times. He served two more beers before coming back over and resuming his conversation with Jack.

"So I heard that you were sick lately. How are you feeling now?"

"Better," Jack told him. "Still a bit sensitive to light and noise, but otherwise, I'm fine."

"Sensitive to noise, eh? I don't think you came to the right place," Bill said as he gestured to the band.

"I'll deal with it."

"Sully! How the hell are ya?" called another voice from across the room. It was Jack's friend Ed, who was seated with Jerry and Shaun, two of the pub's regulars. Jack got up and shook their hands in warm greeting. "Haven't seen ya in some time. What have you been up to?"

"I was sick for a while, then was in New York."

"What were you doing in New York?" Ed asked.

"Oh, some guy sent me there to purchase an old steamer trunk that I had located for him. It used to belong to some famous magician."

"Like Harry Houdini?" Jerry interceded.

"Not quite that famous, but close, I guess."

"So what are you working on now?" asked Ed. "Brion was hoping that you'd have some time to do more work on his family tree."

A couple of weeks earlier, one of their friends, Brion, had hired Jack to trace his family tree back a few more generations than he already had. Jack proved to be quite successful in this task, but knew that there was the chance to go back even further. This was just before he got sick.

"Brion's going to have to wait a little," Jack informed them. "I'm afraid that I've already got something else cooking right now."

"Is it that cursed rag doll?" asked Shaun, who had remained silent until now.

"No. It's something a little bigger than that. But it's funny that you should bring that up. I just got a reply to a query that I had posted about it on one of the sites I regularly use. Someone may have found it in Traer County, Iowa: right where I thought it would be."

"Well that's good," said Shaun.

"So you'll be going to Iowa soon?" asked Positive Bill as

54

he pulled out another beer for Jerry.

"Perhaps. It depends on how long this other case takes."

"This must be some case," Ed declared. "You've been looking for that rag doll for the better part of three years now. I'd have thought you'd be off in a heartbeat to get it."

"So what *are* you working on right now?" Jerry asked the question that was on everybody's mind. They were a little too hesitant to ask though. It wasn't like Jack to pass up on something as monumental as the rag doll that had monopolized so much of his time.

"Sorry guys," Jack said. "I can't talk about this one. Not right now, at least. I'll tell you all about it though once it's over with."

The others were a bit put out, but understood. There were cases in Jack's past that were dependent on secrecy. In the end though, it was always worth it. The stories that he'd tell them were almost unbelievable. Had they been coming from someone else, they certainly would have been, but then it was Jack, and he was always full of surprises.

A moment later, the door to the back patio opened and in walked Amy, one of Jack's oldest friends.

Jack and Amy had first met back in the sixth grade when they were paired up as lab partners in science class. In truth, neither thought very much of the other at first, but after a time, they became very close. As it turned out, both had quite a bit in common: especially in the area of creative writing. Many a story was written between them in study hall. Following their high school years, they would get together for coffee and continue to write. As they entered their early twenties, the location for these story sessions was shifted to the local pub. But as with most things in life, the stories began to dwindle and the ideas started to dry up. True, Jack had continued to write, but he'd become more focused on nonfiction while Amy had immersed herself more into her work. She now owned an apothecary and occult bookstore called The Slivey Toves: an homage to Lewis Carroll's *Jabberwocky*. The store took up most of Amy's time and energy. The fact that she was out this late had surprised Jack greatly. She was usually home by ten.

"You're back!" Amy exclaimed as she caught sight of Jack

across the room. She came over and threw her arms about him. She certainly was a very physical individual. "When did you get home?"

"Yesterday morning," Jack replied.

"And you didn't call?"

"I've been busy."

"New case," Jerry interjected.

Amy took a long, hard look at Jack.

"And something tells me that you're not going to tell us about it, are you?" she said.

"Not yet. I will when it's over with though. I promise."

"Well," Amy said as she took a step back, "the rest of us are outside on the patio. Why don't you come out and join us?"

"The rest of us?" Jack asked.

"Yeah: Joe, Geoff and Chad. I'm sure they'd be more than happy to see you."

Jack nodded, picked up his glass and stepped out into the cool autumn night air.

Jack had known Amy almost as long as he had known Joe and Geoff. He'd first met Joe in the winter of fourth grade, shortly after Joe had moved into the house across the street from his own. At first, the two absolutely hated each other. Joe had been hanging out with Dave, a guy that lived up the street. One afternoon there was a snowball fight and Joe had called Jack's older sister, Lynn, a prostitute. He had quite a mouth on him for a fourth grader. At hearing this, Jack loaded a snowball with a small rock and threw it at Joe. It hit him square in the face and broke his glasses.

The following summer, the two found themselves skateboarding on the street in front of their houses at the same time. After a while, they began to talk and the rest, as they say, is history.

Geoff, on the other hand, became friends with Jack at once. Following the fourth grade, Jack's parents pulled him out of Catholic school and placed him and his brother Michael in the public elementary school at the end of their street. While waiting in line to go inside on that first day of class, Jack struck up a conversation with the boy standing in front of him. As it turned out, Geoff was quite easy to talk to and always seemed eager to laugh. Over the following years, they would both earn the reputation of being the class clowns.

Chad was a relatively new friend. Jack had met him a couple of years earlier when he had first started going into McNamara's. They both enjoyed a Guinness and a Jameson's and were both into Irish music and mariner shanties. An odd coincidence in all of this was that Chad now sailed as a merchant marine for the same company that Jack had once worked for. An even greater coincidence was the surprise that Jack had when he moved into his apartment on Hathaway Avenue a few months later. Chad, as it turned out, lived in the house next door.

Jack sat outside with his friends and took in the cool atmosphere of the season. They told stories, reminisced and joked around about old times. They caught up on what everyone was up to these days and simply enjoyed each others' company. Jack never once hinted at the case he was working on and no one asked. They knew they'd hear about it at some point.

It was evenings like this that made Jack feel like the richest man on Earth. He was glad to be back home in Cleveland.

Three hours, four Guinness' and two Jameson's later, Jack walked out of McNamara's. As he approached his black Mazda Protegé 5, he noticed a tan Ford Focus sitting across the street from him, the engine running and the parking lights on. He tried not to look directly at it, as he didn't want the car's occupant to know that he'd been spotted. The driver was obviously watching him. Jack started his car, put it in gear and pulled out onto Lake Avenue. As he pulled up to the light at Lake and Clifton, he saw the car slowly pulling up behind him. The light changed and Jack turned left onto Clifton. The car followed. It was three miles to Jack's street and the Focus never left his tail. As Jack pulled onto Hathaway Avenue, he looked into his rear-view mirror and saw that the car had broken off its pursuit. He turned into his driveway and stepped out of his car, quite confused as to who it was that had just followed him.

Chapter 8

The first thing that Jack did the following morning was place a call to his cousin Trish. He had thought considerably about something that Shelby had said to him the previous evening: something about using unorthodox methods. Enlisting Trish's assistance would be about as unorthodox as he could get.

Jack had first met Trish a few years earlier while he was helping out a paranormal investigative group with a project at a house called Killington Hill in Southern Ohio. He had been brought in to help solve a mystery concerning a young woman that had died unexpectedly around 1890. Legends maintained that she had been killed after being pushed from a balcony. After a bit of research, Jack found this to be false. She had actually died from consumption: an archaic term for pulmonary tuberculosis.

While staying at Killington Hill, Jack had befriended one of the property managers: a woman in her late forties. They found themselves talking one afternoon while Jack was busy at work on his family tree. The manager always had an affinity for genealogy, so Jack decided to show her some basic methods for researching one's ancestors. As he brought up different pages, some of the names that Jack rattled off began to sound a bit familiar to her. It wasn't until Jack had named his great, great grandfather that the manager knew why. That was the same name as her grandfather's eldest brother. When Jack learned her grandfather's name, he cross-referenced it with what he had. It was a match. Coincidence had introduced Jack to Trish: his second cousin, twice removed.

Trish was what many people would consider "gifted". Back in school though, she was constantly referred to as "a freak". This was many years ago and she had since gotten well past all of the name-calling. As it turned out, children could be quite cruel; especially when dealing with something that they couldn't understand. She had an uncanny ability to find things that were missing: a book, a set of car keys or even a piece of jewelry for example. That could easily have been explained away as intuition. However, Trish knew things about people's pasts: things that they never talked about. One day, when she was about thirteen, a friend had asked her how she could possibly know so much about people's pasts. That's when Trish revealed that she could, on occasion, see people who had passed on. Any credibility that she had before then went right out the window. Everyone figured that she was delusional and from then on would hardly even talk to her.

As she entered college though, she began to take part in studies and it turned out that she scored quite high on what was termed "the extra-sensitivity scale". She had been encouraged to pursue a career in psychology, but by this point, she was more interested in getting her degree in business management. Maintaining that old property in southern Ohio turned out to be her dream job. She could run a successful business and still use her abilities where they would be effective. After all, who better to manage a haunted house than a psychic medium with a business degree?

The phone continued to ring until Trish's voicemail picked up.

"You've reached Trish Martin. I'm unable to answer my phone right now, but if you leave your name and a message, I'll call you back as soon as I can."

After the tone, Jack began to speak.

"Hi, Trish. It's Jack. It's about nine thirty on Friday morning..."

There was a beep. For a second Jack thought that his message had stopped recording, but when he looked at his phone, he saw that Trish was calling him back already. He hit the "talk" button.

"Hello?" he asked.

"Jack? It's Trish. Sorry I didn't get to the phone in time. It was buried in the bottom of my purse"

"That's okay. How have you been?"

"I've been okay. Things have been really busy though for the past few weeks."

"Really?"

"Yeah, you know, Halloween coming up and all that. We always have the place booked solid this time of the year. What have you been up to?"

"Quite a bit, actually. I was out with the flu for about a week and just got back from New York."

"New York? Did you have a good time?" she asked.

59

"Yeah, it was alright."

"Glad to hear it. So to what do I owe the pleasure of your call? Are you thinking of driving down for a visit? I could clear a room for you if you are."

"Na, I'm kind of busy right now with another case. Actually, I was wondering if you'd be able to come up and give me a hand with it; if only for a day or two."

"I swear that sometimes I think you have the gift as well."

"Why's that?"

"Because I'm on my way up right now."

"Oh," Jack acknowledged with a hint of surprise.

"Yeah, I'm supposed to get together with my sister for dinner this evening."

"What about the house? Don't you have any groups coming in tonight?"

"George can take care of them. What case are you working on?"

"I'd rather wait to tell you about it when I see you. There's a lot to it. What time do you think you'll be in town?"

"I should be there in another hour. Do you want to meet at your house?"

"That sounds fine. I just need to straighten things up a little. This place is something of a mess."

"Alright then. I'll see you in about an hour."

"Right. Drive safe."

"Thanks."

Jack hung up the phone. A moment later it rang again with the telephone number coming up as "*unknown*". He hit the "*talk*" button only to hear a recorded voice telling him that if he was satisfied with his message he should press "*one*". He hung up the phone thinking about how some technologies had become redundant.

After taking a shower, dressing himself, loading the dishwasher and cleaning the cat boxes, Jack sat at his desk and booted up his laptop. It was always a good idea, he thought, to have it ready, just in case there was something that needed to be looked up at a moment's notice. He glanced at the clock on the wall; it was now ten thirty. Trish would be there any minute, so there wasn't enough time for him to go the gas station for a cup of coffee. He checked his email and was about halfway through a pretty lame joke that his father had sent him when he heard a knock at the door.

"Come on up," he announced as he deleted the email and closed his mailbox. The door opened and closed. Trish made her way up the stairs and into his living room. Jack walked over to her and gave her a hug. "It's good to see you again."

"Yeah, you too. I'm glad I got here when I did. It looks like it's about to storm."

"Huh?" Jack walked over to the window where Aislinn was sitting and saw that the sky to the north was growing quite dark. A moment later, the wind picked up and it began to rain.

"Wow, that was close," he exclaimed.

"To make matters worse, I left my umbrella back at Killington Hill."

"Looks like it'll pass in a few minutes, but if its still raining when you leave, you're welcome to use mine."

"Oh, I don't want to take your umbrella."

"That's okay. I've got another one out in the car."

"Well, thanks. So what's the project that you're working on?"

Jack filled her in on all that had transpired over the last few days: how he had met Shelby Tomlinson and what had happened to her fifteen years earlier. He told her about the cases of the other girls around Cleveland and those that had gone missing in the other states. He showed her the newspaper articles and the notes that he had taken while interviewing Lauren Call-Ferris. Trish took this all in and quietly listened until he had completed his briefing.

"So, what do you think?" Jack asked her as he finished.

"I think you've got just about everything you need right here."

"Are you getting any immediate impressions from any of this?"

"Well, Jack, it doesn't quite work that way. I would do better to see something more tangible. You don't happen to have anything that once belonged to any of these girls, do you?"

"I'm afraid not."

"And it wouldn't be possible to visit a house that any of

them lived in."

"I don't think so." Jack thought about this for a second. "How about a place where one of them was abducted?"

"That might work," Trish agreed. "I mean, it's always worth a try."

Jack pulled out the map of greater Cleveland that he had marked up two nights earlier. He noticed immediately that he hadn't amended the location of where Lauren was attacked. He quickly scribbled out the circle that he had made on Alameda and drew a new one on Westerly.

"Just making a correction," he told Trish. "Now, these all look pretty vague as far as exact locations go." Jack scanned the map and saw the spot where number four, Nadine Somerset, had gone missing from Terrace Hill. It was a small mark on Brunswick Street. She had vanished somewhere between home and her friend's house, just a few doors away. Jack pointed it out to Trish. "This looks to be our best bet," he told her. She agreed and with that, Jack turned off his laptop, gathered his notebook and binder and they were off. As he had hoped, it had stopped raining.

They pulled onto the 3200 block of Brunswick Street and parked the car at the side of the road. Jack had only been to Terrace Hill once before and that was many years ago, when he was about twelve or thirteen. It was for his father's annual company picnic that was held at the CEO's estate. He remembered swimming in the pool and spending much time talking with his father's boss' daughter: a beautiful girl his age with long blonde hair. From what he could remember, this area was mostly rural. He now found himself in a suburban neighborhood though. It wasn't quite what he was expecting.

Jack pulled out his notebook and found the page where he had written down Nadine Somerset's address: 3217 Brunswick. He and Trish stepped out of the car and began to walk up the street. After a few minutes, they found the house. There was nothing extraordinary about it. It looked much like the other colonial style homes that were on the street. It had a large front yard, was two stories high, had light blue vinyl siding and needed a new roof.

"This is it," Jack told Trish.

"Hmm," she grunted as she stared at the house. She looked down at the sidewalk for a moment and began walking south.

"Have you picked up on something?"

"I'm not a bloodhound," she informed Jack. "But yes, I think I'm feeling something here."

They continued to walk for a few moments and stopped outside of a house eight doors south of where the Somersets had lived.

"What is it?" Jack asked.

"This is where she started from." Trish turned around and started walking north again. They passed five houses and Trish suddenly stopped cold. She crouched down and touched her hand to the sidewalk for a moment. As she lifted it back up, Jack could see that there were tears streaming down her face.

"Are you okay?"

"This is where it happened," she said through sobs. Jack placed a hand on her shoulder.

"It's alright." He first looked over at the house they had just been standing in front of and then over at the Somerset house. "She was so close to home."

"I know," Trish told him as she stood up and dried her eyes. "Her head is hurting and she's looking at her house. Everything looks like it's flashing. She can't hear anything and she can't talk. She's reaching out for her house but someone is grabbing her hands. Someone bigger than her... a man. He now has her legs too and is picking her up. She can't see her house anymore, only the inside of a car. She's staring at the back of a seat. Her head and the side of her face feel dirty, like she's all covered in mud. He's touching her shoulder now. He's rolling her over now..."

Trish gasped and dropped to her knees. She placed her hand again on the sidewalk but quickly recoiled it as though the pavement had burned her. She stood back up, tried to catch her breath and began to pace about.

"It's okay, Trish. Trish! Stop! It's okay! It's over. It happened a long time ago."

He grabbed Trish by the shoulders and held her at arm's length until she regained her composure. She was still quite shaken when she looked back up at Jack.

"That's not it," she told him quietly.

"What then?"

Trish took a few more deep breaths and thought it best to sit back down on the sidewalk. It no longer hurt to touch it. She rubbed the palms of her hands over her eye sockets and cleared the tears. She glared back up at Jack with a horrified look.

"...I saw his face."

Chapter 9

"I want you to describe him to me."

Jack and Trish were sitting back in the car, which was still parked on the side of Brunswick Street. Jack had pulled out his notebook and a pen and was going to do his best to make something of a police sketch based off of what she could tell him. He wasn't that bad of an artist, but when it came to drawing people, he always felt that they looked too "cartoonish".

"He has a round sort of head with thinning hair."

"Okay," Jack said as he began to sketch.

"His eyes are small, but he has bushy eyebrows."

"Can you see what color his eyes are?"

"No. Nor can I tell you the color of his hair."

"Okay, go on."

"His nose is slightly bulbous."

"Like this?" Jack asked as he held up the sketch.

"No. Rounder. And his chin is round too."

"Round chin. What about his mouth?"

"He's wearing a frumpy expression."

"Like he's pouting?"

"No. Like he's agitated."

Jack continued to draw for a few more moments. He wanted to make sure that he got everything down to the best of his ability. When he was satisfied, he held up the picture.

"Something like this?"

"Kind of. Here, let me see it."

Trish took the notepad and pen from Jack and began to modify the drawing.

"His ear lobes were connected at the bottom. He also has a goatee."

Jack remembered the goatee from the other descriptions, but didn't put it in the drawing nor did he mention it to Trish. He figured that he'd take a page out of what Sheriff's Deputy Lauber had told him about withholding some information to validate the legitimacy of a tip. It wasn't that Jack had ever doubted Trish's abilities, he just wanted to see if she would get it on her own.

"There," said Trish as she handed the drawing back to Jack.

"That's him, or at least as good as I could do."

Jack looked long and hard at the drawing.

"What was he wearing?" he asked.

"Huh? Oh, a heavy coat and a scarf."

"Like a parka?"

"No, more like a wool overcoat. It was black, I think."

"Was he wearing any gloves?"

Trish closed her eyes for a moment and tried to remember what she saw when the girl was being picked up.

"Yes," she said at last. "He had gloves on. They were leather. Also black, I believe."

Jack quickly wrote this down in the margin beside the picture. He took one more look at the drawing before he closed the book.

"So where do you think he took her?" Jack wanted to continue with this while these images were still fresh in her mind. Trish closed her eyes for a few moments. When she opened them again, she looked over at Jack very apathetically.

"West. They traveled west."

It was getting later in the day and the wind had picked up considerably since they had left Jacks house that morning. It had sprinkled a few times since then, but not nearly as hard as it had right after Trish had arrived. The two had been driving around for a couple of hours now, going down side streets and through rural areas. Jack was thoroughly lost at this point and was beginning to think that Trish had lost the feeling.

"I don't have to be psychic to know what you're thinking," she said after nearly ten minutes of silence. "You think I don't know where I'm going."

"Okay. You're right. Do you really think he would have driven around for two hours with an abducted eleven-year-old girl on the back seat of his car? She'd have regained consciousness by now."

"Jack, where have we gone since leaving Terrace Hill?"

"I honestly don't know. I'm just following your directions."

"And we've changed direction a few times since leaving there. Haven't we?"

"Yeah, I guess so."

"I'm being drawn to the places where the other girls went missing from."

"Really?" Jack hadn't noticed it, but they did seem to be circling one general area. "Why didn't you want to stop?"

"I don't need to. I know how he operates now. I know what he looks like and I don't think we need to go through another episode like the one back there again."

"True," Jack said with a slight hint of relief. "So where are we going now?"

"I think I know where he took them. Stay on this road for a few more minutes. We'll be turning left soon."

Jack did as he was instructed. They continued driving down the road until Trish suddenly grabbed his shoulder.

"This is it," she announced at last. "Stop the car!"

Jack applied the brakes until the car gently came to a halt at the side of the road. He put it into park and looked out his window.

"So?" Jack asked as he awaited her next instruction.

"No. This is all wrong," she told him.

"What's all wrong?"

"None of this feels right."

Jack looked out the window to his left and saw a newer housing development. The sign at the entrance said *Fleur-de-lis Estates*.

"So now what?"

"We keep going. Turn left down this first street, but drive slowly."

He put the car back into gear, turned on his left turn signal and slowly entered the development on a street called Marseilles Lane. They continued on for two blocks before Trish told him to hang a right. He complied. They drove past a few houses when Trish instructed him to stop the car again.

"This is it," she announced, a hint of excitement in her voice.

"This house can't be more than ten years old."

"I know, but this is it. Trust me."

"Okay, let's have a look then."

They both stepped out of the car. It looked like it was

67

about to start raining again, so Jack brought his umbrella with him. He also picked up his notebook in case they found something worth writing down. They slowly strolled up the driveway, looking about as if some clue were ready to jump out at them. Trish began to walk into the back yard. Jack followed and could see that along the back stood a privacy fence. Beyond the fence was a patch of woods. Sitting in the center of the yard was an above ground swimming pool with a deck attached.

"This still doesn't feel right," Trish told him.

"What doesn't feel right about it?"

"Everything. It feels so close, yet so far away. Something about this place though tells me that the man we're looking for has been here.

"Can I help you?" asked an astonished voice from behind them. They both turned to find themselves confronted by a woman in her late sixties standing by the house.

"Good afternoon," Jack began.

"What are you doing in my yard?" she interrupted.

"I'm sorry," continued Jack. "We were wondering if you could help us."

"If you wanted my help you'd have come to the front door."

"True, but…"

"Well, what is it?"

Jack suddenly remembered the drawing in his notebook. He quickly pulled it out.

"We were wondering if you had seen this man."

Trish lightly jabbed him in the bicep. She didn't approve of his bluntness.

"Hmm. Let's have a look there."

Jack handed her the sketch they had made earlier. She studied it for a few minutes and handed it back.

"Not a very good drawing," she told Jack with a sneer.

"Thank you. Does he look at all familiar though?"

"No. I've never seen this man before, but he does look like that idiot that works at the bank."

"The bank?" Jack said nonchalantly.

"How long have you lived here?" Trish abruptly asked.

"Eight years now."

"Are you the original owner?" she continued.

"No. I bought it in 99' and the house was built in 96'. The original owner only lived here for a couple of years before he moved away."

There was a long pause in the conversation as the elderly woman eyed Jack and Trish with suspicion.

"That's a nice pool," Trish added.

"Came with the house. Not much good in the winter, but in the summer, it does wonders for my arthritis. Is there anything else?"

"No, thank you," Jack said. He turned to Trish and stared at her as if telling her that they best get going.

"Hope I was able to help," the woman told them as they walked back up the driveway. Jack could tell that she was being sarcastic.

"Nice pool?" he quietly asked Trish.

"I couldn't think of anything else to say."

After Jack and Trish had arrived back at Jack's place, Trish made haste to leave. As it was, she would be quite late in meeting up with her sister for dinner. She had invited Jack to join them, but he still had much to do. Besides, Shelby was expected over again that evening. This piqued Trish's interest as she had many times in the past attempted to play matchmaker for Jack. He assured her that it was strictly business between them. Trish didn't seem so sure. She simply called it "a feeling she had".

Jack walked up into his apartment, set his coat down and scooped up Fionn. Aislinn, as usual, was sitting in the window, a look of disdain about her. After booting up his laptop and setting Fionn down, Jack walked over to the refrigerator and grabbed a porter from the dwindling six-pack. There were now only two left. He'd have to run to the store before long. Besides that, there was hardly a scrap of food in the house. He'd have to come up with something later on for dinner.

Jack sat for a few hours at his computer checking his email and looking up a few things on a genealogy website for his mother. Soon, it was dark outside. After a time, he had dozed off. He awoke to a knock at the door below.

"Come on up," he announced as he snapped out of his coma.

He knew immediately that it was Shelby. He hadn't noticed it the first few times, but she always seemed to be accompanied by the slightest scent of patchouli. If worn in excess, it could be quite overpowering. Shelby, though, seemed to find the right balance.

"How did it go today?" she asked as she pulled up her regular stool beside him.

"Not too bad. We were quite productive."

"We?"

"Well, you mentioned that I use unorthodox methods, so I used one today and called my cousin Trish in to help me with this."

"And was she able to help?"

"Like you wouldn't believe."

Jack pulled out his notebook and turned to the page that contained the drawing of the kidnapper. He handed it to Shelby who looked at it for a long time. It was hard for Jack to read the expression on her face.

"Does he look familiar at all?" Jack asked at last. Shelby closed her eyes for a moment.

"Yes. This is him, isn't it?"

"We believe so."

"And where did you get this from?"

"Trish. She's what we consider 'gifted'."

"How gifted?"

"Gifted enough to lead me to my next clue. We just came back from a house out in Greeley Township that she's certain is connected to this man."

"So… how do you find out for certain?"

"Modern technology," he told her as he turned to his laptop. "I'm starting with the county auditor's website."

Jack typed in a few keywords on his computer, brought up the website and filled in the address information. He clicked the "enter" button on his keyboard and it brought up a new screen.

"What's this tell us?" Shelby asked.

"Well, It gives us the name of the woman that owns the house we just visited. Here it is: Laverne Quinstead. Whoops!"

"What is it?" Shelby asked with astonishment.

"Mrs. Quinstead is behind on her taxes."

"And this helps us how?"

"Well, it doesn't. But it says here whom she purchased the property from: one Mr. Vincent Arndt."

"Who's Vincent Arndt?"

"Let's find out."

Jack brought up his digital white pages, but could find no Vincent Arndt listed anywhere in the area.

"I have another thought," He added as he brought up another website. "This is the Cleveland Necrology File, provided as a courtesy of the Cleveland Public Library. It lists abstracts of everyone who died in the area between 1850 and 1975. Anything after that, we go to this link below. It's the Cleveland News Index." Jack clicked on it and entered the name "Arndt".

"Here it is," he announced. "Arndt, Vincent D., Age 39, Beloved husband of Maggie... damn."

"What?"

"It's dated from four years ago. This can't be him. He'd have been 28 when you were abducted: about fifteen years too young."

"Oh."

"Don't give up yet. I have another idea."

"What's that?"

"We do a property trace."

"A property trace on what?"

"The property in Greeley Township that Trish and I just visited. I'm going to the Cuyahoga County Recorder's website to find this."

"Why on the property? Didn't you say that it was the *house* that was the connection?"

"Yes, but maybe it's the property itself. The house might be coincidental."

Jack typed in a few keywords again, clicked "*enter*" and in a moment he had found it. He entered the pertinent dates along with the names "Arndt" and "Vincent" where they applied and clicked his mouse. A new screen came up and Jack studied it for a few moments.

"Is there anything there?" Shelby asked.

"Some. I'm looking for a few names... and... here it is."

Jack clicked the mouse a couple more times, brought up a few more screens and a moment later was printing out a form.

"What's that?"

"It's the title transfer from Mr. Arndt to Mrs. Quinstead. It's dated from March of 1999. This will give us a full description of the parcel of land in question."

"What do you mean?"

"Well, the only keyword mentioned is the word '*Rainey*'. Let's see what that says." Jack studied the page closely and soon found what he was looking for. "Look here," Jack said as he held the form in front of her. "It says Lot Number 45 of Rainey's Sub-division, from part of lot 15 of the Markson Purchase, dated June 12, 1828, from Original Lots 31 and 32 of the Seventh Township in the Tenth Range of the Connecticut Western Reserve. That's our key."

"So what do we do now?"

"We look for this in Mr. Arndt's column and see who he purchased it from."

"How do we do that?"

"Same way we did the last one. We just look for 'Rainey' again as the property description."

Jack clicked the mouse a few pages back and began sorting through the files.

"Anything?"

"Yeah… it says here that he purchased the land from the Calgaine Building Company."

"Who are they?"

"A housing development firm, I think. They must have been the ones who built his house back in the late nineties."

"Who'd *they* buy it from?"

"Good question." Jack continued to stare at the laptop as he clicked through multiple screens. It wasn't long before he found what he was looking for. "There it is," he told her.

"There *what* is?"

"Stuart Shipping and Handling"

"Who's that?"

"No Idea, but it looks like they owned the land before Calgaine did."

"How long did they own it for?"

72

"One sec… I'm finding that out now." Jack clicked a few more times and delivered the answer. "Looks like they owned it between July of 1990 and November of 1996."

"So they're the ones who owned it back when I was abducted?"

"Would appear so."

"Hey, do you remember what we had talked about the other night?"

"What part?" Jack asked as he turned around to face her.

"About possible occupations of the guy who kidnapped me. Remember? We had brought up night watchman… when we'd been talking about someone who carries a large flashlight."

"That's right. I think it's worth looking into. I'll try to locate them in the morning and see if they're even still around. As it is, there are a couple of other places I need to run to." Jack jotted a few quick entries into his notebook and closed the windows on his laptop. "Have you eaten dinner yet?"

"Huh?"

"I was thinking of ordering a pizza from Angelo's. Do you like pepperoni?"

"No, thank you. I'm not hungry. In fact, I should be going."

Jack looked out the window and saw that it was raining again.

"Can I offer you an umbrella? It's pouring."

"I'll be alright. Can I see you again tomorrow evening?"

"Tomorrow evening would be fine, but let's meet a little later. I have some running around to do and I'm not sure when I'll be home." Jack found with astonishment that he was looking forward to seeing her again. Perhaps there was something to what Trish had said after all.

"What time were you thinking?"

"How does eleven sound?"

"Eleven is fine."

Jack looked out the window again. The rain showed no signs of letting up.

"Let me at least walk you to your car."

"That's okay," she told him as she stood up to leave. "I'm not going far."

As Jack heard the front door below click shut, he looked out the front window and saw her walking up the street through the rain. He felt bad. She wasn't even wearing a coat. Jack couldn't take it. He quickly grabbed the umbrella, ran down the stairs and out the front door.

"Shelby!" he called after her through the pouring rain, but the street was empty. She had already driven away.

As planned, Jack had ordered a pizza with double pepperoni. All things considered, he was a pretty good cook. His friends raved constantly about his Guinness beef, president's chicken and Louisiana style barbecue. As of late though, he hadn't felt much like cooking.

After downing five slices of pizza, and another bottle of porter, Jack went up to McNamara's to meet a few of his friends. It was a fairly uneventful night, even though it was a Friday. Apparently, most of the regulars had overdone it the night before and were lying low that evening. Jack decided to call it an early night as well. He was home by eleven. To his relief, he wasn't followed this time.

Normally, he would have been online again or goofing around on his guitar. Something told him though that he should watch the news and catch up on what had been happening in the world. He wasn't disappointed. The lead story was about an arrest being made in connection with the disappearance of Rebecca Lowe. The suspect in custody was a man named Milton Adams, a 36-year-old registered sex offender that lived on the next street. When they flashed his face upon the screen, Jack was quite certain, they had the wrong man.

Chapter 10

As soon as Jack awoke, he got on the phone with Trish to tell her about what he had seen last night on the news. She had seen it too and definitely agreed with him that they had the wrong man in custody. Not only was he the wrong age, but he also looked nothing like the man that Trish had described the previous day. Jack wondered if he should go to the sheriff's department and tell them what he knew. Trish, however, dissuaded him from doing this. As far as they were concerned, he was off this case.

They agreed to meet for breakfast at Diana's on West 117th Street to discuss what Jack had found online the night before. He was going to have a busy day and could definitely use a good meal before starting out.

The rain had cleared out during the middle of the night and the skies were sunny once more. It would be a beautiful Saturday for doing some running around. Usually, Jack would stay in for the first part of the morning watching cartoons until around ten. After that, he'd run his errands: grocery shopping, banking, car wash, hardware store... if there was something around the house that needed fixing. To pass the time while driving, he'd listen to NPR; usually *Whad'Ya Know?* with Michael Feldman and *Wait Wait... Don't Tell Me!* With Peter Sagal and Carl Kasell. He could still catch parts of his radio shows, but he'd have to pass on the cartoons.

As he stepped out of his car at Diana's, he noticed Trish's Malibu parked across the lot. She had beaten him there and he began to wonder how long she had been waiting. He walked in and saw her sitting at a small table across the room. The hostess stopped him at the door and attempted to seat him, but he politely let her know that his party was already present and expecting him. He crossed the room and pulled up a chair at the table where his cousin sat.

"Sorry to keep you waiting," he told her.

"Oh, that's okay. I just got here myself a few minutes ago."

The waitress came over and took their beverage orders.

They were both having coffee.

"So what *should* I do about all of this," he asked.

"I wouldn't do anything at the present," replied Trish. "Stick with your investigation into the earlier disappearances and find out as much as you can. I have a feeling that this will lead you to the real killer."

"That's interesting."

"What?"

"You just referred to him as a killer. We don't know that he's killed anyone yet."

"Come on, Jack. These girls have been missing for fifteen years now. I'm pretty sure that they're not vacationing in sunny Orlando."

"But no bodies have been recovered yet. I'm just saying that it's premature to classify him as a killer."

As Jack said this, the waitress had walked up to take their food orders. She caught the end of what he had said and was visibly uncomfortable. Trish ordered the Belgian waffle and Jack was having two eggs over medium with bacon and toast. He was a pretty bad Irishman as far as some things were concerned. He didn't care much for potatoes and rarely ordered them, especially with breakfast.

"So what did you find out last night?" asked Trish after taking a few sips from her coffee.

"Well, the guy that the old lady had bought the house from has been dead for the last four years. He'd have been too young to be our kidnapper anyway. He purchased it directly from the building company who originally picked up the land from a company called Stuart Shipping and Handling. They're the ones who owned it during the time that the girls went missing."

"What did they use the land for?"

"I don't know. I'm going to see what I can find on them today."

"Jack, it's Saturday. Do you think they'll be open?"

"I don't even know if they're still around. That's what I have to find out first."

They sipped their coffee in silence for a few minutes before Jack spoke up again.

"Oh. How was dinner with your sister?"

"Not bad. She's working all weekend."

"I'll be honest with you. That's one job that I'd never want; no matter how much you paid me."

"And they pay Pam quite well."

"Still Trish, the morgue? That would bother the hell out of me."

"That would bother you? The same guy who spends all this time researching haunted houses and collecting cursed items? They're just dead people. It's not like they can hurt you or anything. I'd be more worried about some of those weird items that you have in your spare room."

Trish was one of the few people that Jack had confided in when it came to the actual contents of his spare room. He didn't share everything with her, just a few items that he had specific questions about. One such item was the ax that Lizzie Borden allegedly murdered her parents with. Stories maintained that the weapon would fill its wielder with an uncontrollable rage. Upon reviewing this item, Trish had suggested that he dispose of it. Jack flatly refused. The only other advice she could give was for him not to handle it.

Their food arrived and everything looked to be in order. Jack salted the daylights out of his plate before starting on his eggs.

"Hey, I just had an idea," he said after swallowing a piece of bacon. "How late is the county morgue open today?"

"Jack, it's a morgue. It's always open. But what's your idea?"

"Shelby told me that none of the Jane Does that came in after late 92' matched any of the missing girls from the area."

"So?"

"Well, I can't help but wonder if any of them might match up with some of the girls that went missing in the other states."

"Do you really think that he would travel half-way across the country with a dead girl in his car just to dump the body somewhere that it wouldn't be identified. For one, think of the smell."

"What if they were still alive?"

"They'd make noise. That and I'm sure he'd have to stop for the night at least once along the way."

"Maybe if he were coming from Flagstaff or San Francisco, but not Pittsburgh. He could make it here in a little less than three hours. He could also do Kansas in a day, if he drove straight through."

"I'm sure that they would have broadened their search after coming up with nothing in the immediate area. Still, you may be onto something. Give me your articles and I'll run them over to Pam this afternoon."

"They're at home. That's okay though. I'll run them over. It'll be good to see her again."

"What about Stuart Shipping and Handling?" Trish asked as she picked up her coffee to finish it off.

"I'll take a look after I get done here. I don't think it'll take that long to find info on them. I also have to pay a courtesy call to one of my clients to see how he's enjoying his new purchase. I can stop at the morgue on my way back through town."

Jack paid their bill and said goodbye to his cousin. Before they parted, she asked him again about Shelby. She could tell that he was starting to see something in her. He maintained that it was just a business relationship and that he didn't get involved with his clients. Trish could tell that he was lying.

After getting back home, booting up his laptop and checking his email, Jack began a search on Stuart Shipping and Handling. His immediate search turned up nothing in the area. He broadened his search and learned that the company had closed many years earlier. After doing a little more research on the subject, he discovered that the owner was a man named Percy L. Stuart, who had recently become a co-owner in another shipping firm. After a few minutes, Jack located his telephone number and gave him a call. The phone rang four times before Percy Stuart picked up.

"Hello, Mr. Stuart?" Jack asked.

"Yes?" The man had the booming voice of a corporate giant.

"My name is John Sullivan and I'm calling in regards to a property that your company once owned out in Greeley Township."

"Greeley Township? I remember that. It was some time

ago, though. What would you like to know about it?"

"Well, I see that your company owned the property from 1990 to 1996."

"That sounds about right."

"I was curious as to what you used the land for."

"Used it? We didn't use it for anything. We'd purchased that land with the hopes of building a large shipping warehouse on the site."

"Why didn't you end up building there?"

"Oh, we had some trouble getting the zoning changed, if I remember right. You see; the whole area was zoned as residential. It was mostly woods though: hardly any houses at all. We ended up moving into another warehouse that had become available out in Solon. Considering that the company folded a few years later, this proved to be much cheaper than building a new facility."

"You said *hardly* any houses?" Jack had an idea.

"Yeah, that's right."

"Were there any structures directly on that property?"

"Come to think of it, there were."

"Such as?"

"Well, there was an old house there. I think it was condemned. There was also a barn. That was probably condemned as well."

"Anything else?"

"Yeah, there was a two-story carriage house. I think there was also an outbuilding or something like that. I had only been out there a few times and like I said, that was some time ago."

"Thank you for taking the time to talk with me about this Mr. Stuart. With your permission, may I call again in the future if I have any more questions?"

"Sure. You wouldn't happen to be a police officer Mr. um, Sullivan is it?"

"No sir. I'm just doing some property research."

"Research?"

"Yeah, I'm a historian… of sorts."

"What sorts?"

"Mostly on properties and hunting down curious items."

"Wait. You're not J. M. Sullivan the author, are you?"

Jack's ego inflated just a bit.

"I am, in fact."

"I have a couple of your books," Mr. Stuart explained. "You don't think that the old house on that property was haunted, do you?"

"No. It's nothing like that. I'm just looking up a few things for a friend."

"I see. Well good luck to you Mr. Sullivan and you have a good day."

"Thank you Mr. Stuart. You too."

Jack hung up the phone. He quickly pulled out his notebook and started to write down what Mr. Stuart had told him about the property: specifically about the condemned buildings that once sat upon it. This merited more research. He quickly went back to the county recorder's website and looked up Stuart Shipping and Handling to see whom they had purchased that piece of land from. It only took a moment for him to find out that the property had belonged to a man named Archibald Swift. When Jack looked him up in the digital white pages, he came up with nothing. He went back to the Cleveland News Index and found him there.

"Swift, Archibald A., 77, Husband of the late Maureen (nee Hubbard)," Jack read aloud. He looked at the date and saw that Mr. Swift had passed away back in 1989. This meant that the Mr. Stuart had actually purchased the property from the executors of Mr. Swift's estate and not Mr. Swift himself.

Jack looked up Mr. Swift's fiduciaries on the county court's website and learned that these were two women. Further research revealed them to be his unwed middle-aged daughters. It was another dead end. Jack looked at the time and realized that the afternoon was wearing on. He needed to get moving if he was going to get all of his running around done.

Jack pulled up the long driveway of Mr. Dresden's estate in Chagrin Falls. It was a beautiful house, flanked by lovely gardens and lush green lawns. Even though the leaves had started to drop from the trees, the yard looked pristine. As Jack stepped out of his car, he noticed Mr. Dresden's chauffeur standing in the garage, wiping a coat of wax from the red Cadillac DTS.

"Good afternoon," Jack announced as he approached.

"Good afternoon, Mr. Sullivan," replied the driver. "To what do we owe the pleasure?"

"Just a courtesy call. I wanted to see how Mr. Dresden was enjoying his recent acquisition."

"Well, he's enjoying it very much I would imagine. It occupies so much of his time that we hardly ever see him."

"Glad to hear it. Is he about?"

"No. I'm afraid that he's out with his daughter for lunch and shouldn't be expected back for a couple of hours. What have you been doing since New York?"

"Actually, I'm working a new case."

"Anything interesting?"

"Missing person's case."

"Oh, like the old man who went missing sixty years ago?"

"A little more recently than that. Some girls that went missing about fifteen years back."

"You don't say."

The driver set down the chamois that he had been wiping the car with and picked up a bottle that looked a lot like rubbing alcohol. He took the cap off and dumped a generous amount on his hands. The smell was atrocious.

"What is that?" asked Jack, slightly repulsed.

"Witch Hazel. My hands get pretty chafed from my driving gloves."

"And that helps?"

"Like you wouldn't believe."

"Smells horrible."

"You get used to it. You know, you really should have called ahead. It would have saved you the trip all the way out here."

"Yeah, I probably should have."

"I'll tell Mr. Dresden that you stopped by though."

"Thanks. You have a good afternoon."

"You too."

Jack got back into his car and drove away. He started to get a few new ideas about this case and how to approach it. Perhaps, he thought, he had been going about it the wrong way. Perhaps he should have been looking for someone who knew the girls: all of them. Maybe there was a common link. It would be difficult trying to find it though. He'd likely have more questions for Shelby that evening. Obviously, he wouldn't be able to talk to the other four girls, but there was always Lauren Call-Ferris. He had written down her phone number when it came up on his caller ID, just in case he needed to ask her more questions. It was a good thing, he thought, that he did.

Jack arrived at the Cuyahoga County Morgue somewhere just before five thirty that afternoon. He parked his car in the visitors lot, walked up to the door and rang the buzzer.

"Yes?" a serious voice called out through a speaker box.

"Pam? It's Jack," he replied.

"Hi Jack." The voice was suddenly much more cheerful and bubbly. "Trish called and told me you'd be coming by."

There was a buzzing sound and Jack instinctively opened the door. The hallway before him was quite dark. The only light he had to go by was coming from behind a partially opened door at the end of the corridor. He had never been to the morgue before and for some odd reason felt slightly nervous. He cautiously approached the door ahead. For a moment, he didn't want to enter. He thought it best to knock perhaps. Barging in might be considered rude, especially if there was some sort of procedure going on. As he raised his fist to wrap upon the steel door, it suddenly flew open and Jack took a leap backwards dropping his file folder.

"Jack! It's great to see you!" his cousin declared with an ecstatic voice. "Sorry. Did I scare you?"

Jack's heart was racing.

"No. Uh. Not at all," he lied.

"Here, you dropped your thing."

She crouched down, picked up the file folder and handed it to him.

"Thanks."

"So, Trish tells me that you're looking into some of our Jane Does. Might have an idea who they are?"

"Possibly," Jack said as he entered the room. It wasn't quite what he had imagined it would be. He'd pictured tables with corpses laid out on them and morticians performing autopsies. To his surprise, it was just a room with a couple of desks and a wall of stainless steel drawers at the far end.

"Not what you were expecting?"

"I guess not," Jack told her.

"Yes, there are dead people here, but they're in those drawers over there... where they can't get you."

"Trish told you then?"

"Of course she told me."

"Great," he said with a slight hint of agitation. "So, where do you..."

"Hack em' up? We have an autopsy room down the hall."

Jack looked back down the corridor he had just come through.

"So you work by yourself?"

"We keep a small staff on the weekends when the main offices are closed, but during the week there can be up to seven or eight of us here at one time. So what have you got for me?"

Jack opened his file folder and handed Pam the newspaper articles that Shelby had sent him.

"They're all missing from different areas of the country," he told her. "Some are from Pittsburgh, some from Flagstaff, some from San Francisco and a few from Kansas. You might have a better hit on Pittsburgh and Kansas."

Pam flipped through the articles as if she would be able to give him an answer right away. He knew this wouldn't be the case.

"So can I hang onto these?" she asked.

"Actually, I'm still actively referencing them. Do you have a copy machine?"

"We sure do."

Pam started to walk over to a photocopier that was sitting across the room beside a set of filing cabinets when there was an abrupt buzzing sound. Jack nearly jumped out of his skin.

"It's okay," she told him. "It's just the door." She set the files down on her desk, walked over to an intercom and pushed the button. "Yes?" she asked in the same serious voice she had used when Jack had first arrived.

"Kollifer's," the voice at the other end announced.

"Hi Bob. Just a sec." Pam pushed a button and Jack could hear a buzzing sound coming from the end of the hallway, followed by the sound of a door slamming shut. A moment later, a middle-aged man had joined them.

"Wasn't expecting you until seven," Pam told the man.

"My meeting ended early," he replied.

"Oh, Bob. I'd like you to meet my cousin, Jack Sullivan. Jack, this is Bob Woodring. He works for Kollifer's Funeral Home."

"Nice to meet you," Jack said as he shook his hand.

"He's over here, Bob," Pam said as she crossed the room and approached the stainless steel drawers. "I'll be just a moment."

"Who's over there?" Jack asked a slight hint of anxiety in his voice.

"Bob's here to make a pick up," she laughed.

Jack took a step back and watched with horror as she opened one of the drawers. Lying on the steel shelf was a long black bag that Jack knew contained human remains. Pam wheeled over a gurney and slid the bag onto it. Jack was scared out of his wits. He looked back over at Bob Woodring who was looking down at the newspaper articles that Pam had set on her desk a minute earlier. Bob shrugged his shoulder at these and looked back up at Pam who was approaching with his parcel and a clipboard.

"Jack, would you be a dear and help Bob with this?" Pam asked as she handed the clipboard to Bob who started to sign it.

"You've got to be kidding me!"

"Jack, please. He's going to need a hand getting him into the van and my back is just about shot." She took the clipboard back and picked up the newspaper articles from her desk. "I'll have these copied by the time you get done."

Jack considered it for a second.

"Alright," he said with a heavy heart.

"You're a lamb," Pam told him as she began to walk to the photocopier. Bob had already started to wheel the gurney down the hall and towards the door. Jack caught up with him as he was exiting the building. Bob stopped the gurney by the tailgate of a minivan that had the words Kollifer's Funeral Home printed on the side. He reached into his pocket, pulled out a key fob and hit a button. The tailgate slowly lifted of its own accord.

"If you want to grab his feet, I'll take the shoulders," Bob instructed. Jack thought to himself that he didn't want to grab anything. Very cautiously though, he grasped a strap by the man's feet.

"Like this?" Jack asked.

"No. Grab his feet. You're not going to hurt him." Jack clammed up a bit as he firmly grabbed at the dead man's feet. "On Three. One... two... three."

They lifted the black bag together and slid it into the back of the van.

"Ugh!" Jack exclaimed.

"That wasn't so bad now. Was it?" Jack leered at him as if telling him to never ask for his help again. "So what do you do for a living, Jack?"

"Huh? Oh, I'm a historian."

"Historian, eh? Does it pay well?"

"Depends, I guess. How long have you worked in the funeral business?"

"Most of my life."

"What's that like?"

"Not as creepy as you would think. It pays pretty well. And remember, you can always count on a mortician. We're the last to let you down."

Jack looked at him funny for a second before he finally got the joke. A moment later, the door opened and Pam emerged with Jack's newspaper articles and his file folder in her hands.

"Here Jack," she said. "I'm done copying these. I'll enter them in the system and see if anything comes up. Might take a few days though."

"Thanks Pam," Jack said as he took the papers from her and tucked them neatly back in the file folder.

"Trish tells me that you might be seeing someone," she added.

"Strictly professional. She's just a client. Speaking of which, I best be on my way. She's supposed to drop by this evening."

"Well, good luck nonetheless."

"Yeah, yeah. I'll see you later. Thanks again." Jack started toward his car but remembered his manners. He turned back towards Bob. "It was nice meeting you," he said as he extended his hand.

"You too," replied Bob with a firm handshake.

Jack got into his car and drove away. It was getting late and the sun was sinking low on the western horizon. The glare began to make his eyes hurt again, so he put on his sunglasses. He stopped at a fast food drive-thru window, picked up a couple of burgers and headed home. Going off of his new theory that the kidnapper might have known all of the girls, Jack would have a lot of questions for Shelby that night.

Chapter 11

Jack usually spent his Saturday nights playing with his band, Whuppity Scoorie, at one of the many fine Irish pubs that Cleveland had to offer. It was a four-piece act with his long-time friend Joe on the drums. Joe was actually an accomplished keyboard player, but was also quite good on percussion. Another friend, Paul, took the leads on his fiddle while their friend Matthew took the bass. Jack wasn't a great guitar player nor was he a great singer, as he sang with what was commonly referred to as something of a "whiskey voice," slightly rough and gravelly. He was proficient enough on a twelve-string guitar though and knew more Irish songs than most. Besides that, he was also a pretty good songwriter. Quite a few of his originals were serious or sad, but lately he'd been writing some pretty funny ones. A couple of them were kind of raunchy. It seemed more and more that this was what the audiences wanted. Not only that, but Jack enjoyed doing it.

As it was, the band was on a slight hiatus for the next few weeks as Matthew was out of town on business and wouldn't be back until the second week of November. He knew that Jack held an incredible Halloween party every year and that he'd miss it, but work was work. The band, which played at this party every year, would have to get by that night without him.

The fact that the band was off that evening really helped Jack to focus on the case he had been working for Shelby. He sat for a few minutes on his couch with his notebook open, trying to figure out what questions he would ask her. He knew that all of the girls involved in this case lived in different cities, so it wasn't likely that they were connected by someone they knew from school: like a teacher or a guidance counselor. Had that been the case, Shelby would have recognized him at once. Perhaps it was someone that knew their families, Jack thought. Again, this didn't seem likely. He began to think that he was wrong in all of this and that there was no connection between these girls at all. Perhaps it was random. Jack thought about it for a few more minutes. He was stumped. He looked up at the clock and saw that it was only a quarter to eight. It would be nearly three hours before Shelby would be over. He decided to take a shower and go up to McNamara's for a couple of beers. Maybe he'd have a better idea of how to approach this new theory later on.

Jack arrived at McNamara's just after eight thirty to find the place packed to the gills. He spent the next two hours hanging out with Joe and Amy who were deep in a conversation about what constituted as *smooth rock*. As near as they could conclude, it would fit best as the soundtrack for someone doing a line of cocaine off a stripper's ass while sailing on a yacht or getting head in a Delorean. Somewhere around nine, Clark, one of the regulars, came in and the conversation for a time was turned to cooking and food. Clark was the owner and executive chef of a bistro in Tremont called The Scranton House. Usually when he came in, if there wasn't a game on, he'd turn the television to a cooking channel and start getting ideas for new dishes that he could prepare.

Jack needed to get some new ideas of his own. Shelby was expected over around eleven and aside from what he'd learned earlier from Percy Stuart, he really didn't have much more to tell her. Perhaps he could ask her a bit about her personal life and get a chance to know her better. Also, he thought, this might be a good way to find out if there was a common link between her and the other girls.

He thought about it for a moment and realized that he might actually be developing feelings for Shelby. This caught him somewhat off-guard. He wasn't the type to fall for a professional colleague or a client.

As ten-thirty approached, Jack realized that he'd just have to stick with the information that Mr. Stuart gave him. With luck, he'd find more tomorrow. He finished off his pint of Guinness, said goodbye to his friends and walked out of the bar. As he approached his car, he noticed the tan Ford Focus sitting across the street. Again, he tried not to stare. He could see someone sitting in the driver's seat, but the person seemed not to be looking at him. He quickly got into his car and drove away. The Focus didn't follow.

Jack found a parking spot directly in front of his house. This was a rarity during the week, as he'd usually have to park about nine or ten houses away. He preferred to leave the driveway open for his first floor neighbor and for guests. Since it was a Saturday evening though, most of his neighbors were out, thus clearing up some room on the street.

He stepped out of the vehicle, slammed the door and locked it with the key fob remote in his pocket. There was a short honk of the horn as he did. The house was completely dark. Corley must have turned off the porch light again, he thought. After all, the switch was in her apartment and it went on her electric bill. Still, it made it harder for Jack to find his front door key. He stood on the darkened porch with his key chain in his hand, trying to find the right one. Suddenly, there was a sharp pain across the back of his neck. Jack went flying forward into the brickwork beside his door. He rolled over onto his back to see a man standing over him with a long object in his hand. He raised it and took another swing but Jack dodged it and the man ended up hitting the concrete of the porch instead. There was a loud cracking sound as he did. Jack kicked out his right leg and caught the man in the gut. He went flying backwards off of the porch and into the front lawn. Jack started to pull himself up. He could tell that his face was bleeding from where it made contact with the wall. The man in the front yard composed himself and charged again. He swung the object in his hand and hit Jack squarely upside the head. Jack collapsed to his knees. He knew he was in trouble. This attacker had a weapon: a clear advantage. There seemed to be no way of him getting help from anyone, but suddenly he remembered the fob on his key chain. The man swung down at Jack again, but he deflected the blow with his left arm. As he did so, he felt his right thumb along the fob until he found the little round button with the exclamation mark and pushed it. His car began to honk furiously with all of the lights flashing in synch. The man took a few steps back and realized that it would be a matter of seconds before one of the neighbors would come out to see what was happening. Perhaps they were already looking out their windows. He looked about and saw that he hadn't been noticed yet. There was still time enough to get away. With that, he took off at a run down the street. Jack collapsed onto his side. His head was throbbing from the blows he'd received and he started to feel dizzy. Everything went dark.

Jack awoke on his couch. His head was propped up with a few pillows and he was covered with the blue and white Indian blanket that usually hung on a rack across the room. His head felt like it was in a vice and the side of his face was stinging. Everything was a haze to him. He suddenly remembered what had happened and quickly sat upright. Instantly, he felt a pair of hands on his shoulders gently pushing him back down to the pillows.

"It's alright," a calming female voice told him. "You're okay now."

Jack looked up to see Shelby sitting beside him.

"How did I get here?" he asked.

"I helped you a bit, but you mostly did it under your own power. You don't remember?"

"No. What happened?"

"You were attacked on your porch. I was coming up the street when I heard a car alarm start to go off. A moment later I saw someone running from your house. That's when I found you unconscious and bleeding. I found your keys and turned off the alarm. You came to for a moment or so and were in and out of it most of the way up the stairs. Did you get a good look at him?"

"No," Jack replied. "Not a good one anyway. It was dark. Did you?"

"No. All I could see was his back as he ran. Actually, he seemed to be lumbering a little, like he had bad knees or something."

"I did kick him in the belly, I think. Maybe I got him in the balls."

"What did he hit you with?"

"I don't know, but it sure as hell hurt."

Jack touched his right hand to the side of his face. It felt like he was wearing a mask.

"I wouldn't touch it," Shelby warned. It's starting to scab up a bit and you don't want to start bleeding again."

Jack wondered for a second if it would scar. He lowered his right hand, put his left one on the back of the couch and began to pull himself up again.

"No, Jack. Stay down."

"I'm okay. I need to sit up." As he said this, he looked

down at his left arm and grabbed it. There was a shooting pain just above his wrist. He pulled up his sleeve and saw that it was swollen and starting to bruise.

"Well, that explains why you were having trouble grabbing the handrail on the way up the stairs." Shelby took a closer look at it. "It doesn't seem to be broken."

"I'm sure it'll be fine. I've got a reusable cold compress in the freezer."

Jack stood up and walked into the kitchen.

"I could have gotten that for you."

"That's okay," Jack told her. "I should probably walk it off anyway. How long was I out?"

"Nearly an hour now."

Jack pulled the cold compress out of his freezer and applied it to his wrist. A numbing pain blasted up his arm. He wiggled his fingers a bit, just to make sure that it wasn't broken. Everything seemed to be working fine: a little stiff, but fine nonetheless.

"I'll be back in a second," he said as he walked toward his bathroom.

He grabbed his terrycloth bathrobe from behind the door and put it on. For a moment, he glanced into the mirror above the sink and saw that the right side of his face was scraped up pretty bad. As Jack reentered the living room, he noticed that Shelby's eyes looked a little puffy. He wondered for a moment if she had been crying.

"So who do you think would have done this?" she asked at last. "Do you have any enemies?"

"None that come to mind."

"This is all my fault."

"Why would you say that?" Jack asked, a slight hint of astonishment in his voice.

"I just can't help but think that you've gotten too close to finding out who the kidnapper is."

"Not likely. I honestly don't have the slightest clue."

"Someone else obviously doesn't think so."

"I really don't think this has anything to do with the case."

"Jack, think about it. Did he demand money?"

"No."

"And if he was just trying to rough you up, he'd have

punched you."

"He did hit me."

"But with a weapon of some sort. A fist injures. If he wouldn't have stopped, he'd have killed you."

Jack considered this for a moment and realized that she was right.

"So someone doesn't want me on this case. The question is who?"

"I think we both know who."

"You think it was him?"

"I have no doubt. Who did you think it was?"

"Well, the sheriff's department has already told me to drop the case."

"I seriously doubt that it was anybody from the sheriff's department."

Jack knew she was right again. She seemed to be making more sense of this than he could.

"So how did he find me?"

"You're really not that hard to find. A better question is, who all knows that you're on this case?"

"Not a lot of people," Jack said as he tried to recall who he had talked to.

"Think for a second."

"I think better when I'm writing." Jack walked over to his desk, picked up his pen and notebook and walked back over to the couch where he took a seat beside Shelby. "There are my cousins, Trish and Pam, but I think we can rule them out right away. There's my friend Maxine, but again, I really don't think she'd be connected to this."

"Who else?"

"Lauren Call-Ferris, her mother-in-law, probably her father-in-law and her husband too, but I didn't see any reason why any of them would want to kill me."

"Yeah, that wouldn't make sense."

"And we've ruled out anyone from the sheriff's department. You know? I did mention this case to the assistant principal at Valleywood High School the other day. Haas I think his name was."

He started to write this down in his notebook.

"That doesn't sound very likely either."

"You're right."

Jack crossed it out.

"Here's another question. Why did he wait until tonight to attack you?"

"I don't know. It was more convenient for him?"

"I don't think so. Did you mention this case to anyone today?"

Jack thought about it for a second.

"Well, Trish and I had breakfast this morning. We were talking about it then. Maybe someone overheard us."

"Again, not likely. I mean, what would be the chances of that?"

"Astronomical, I guess."

"Anyone else?"

"Yeah," Jack remembered. "I spoke this morning to Percy Stuart."

"Who's that?"

"That's what I was going to tell you about tonight. He's the man that owned the company that used to own the property out in Greeley Township back when you were abducted. He said that they never used the property for anything though. They were going to build a warehouse out there but ended up selling the land off."

"And you talked to him today?"

"Yeah. Shelby, there used to be a house and a barn on that property. Does any of this seem familiar to you in any way?"

Shelby closed her eyes and thought about it. A moment later, she opened them and looked at Jack.

"It doesn't. I'm sorry Jack."

"Hmm," Jack thought for a moment. "There's something else."

"What's that?"

"Mr. Stuart knew who I was."

"How?"

"Apparently, he owns a couple of my books."

"Well, I'd definitely keep him in mind. Was there anybody else?"

"That's it... no... wait." Jack thought for a moment.

"There was one other person that I mentioned it to, but…"

"Who Jack?"

"I can't believe I didn't see it earlier."

"What?"

Jack shook his head for a moment and continued.

"I stopped by one of my client's houses this afternoon, but he was out."

"So?"

"So his driver was in."

"His driver?"

"Yeah. He fits the age. He's definitely strong enough to have overpowered me out there. He drives a luxury car and has connections to money. Oh my god!

"What?"

"That smell. Shelby, he was dumping something on his hands called Witch Hazel. Have you ever heard of it?"

"It's a plant, right?"

"I think so, but it also comes in a liquid form."

"So?"

"So it has a very strong chemical smell to it."

Shelby took all of this in for a moment.

"You said he's a driver?" she asked.

"That's right."

"Well, he'd certainly have access to a chauffeur's uniform. Remember what Lauren Call had said about what her attacker was wearing?"

"I remember."

"You said he drives a luxury car?"

"Yeah, a Red Cadillac DTS. I just can't help but wonder if he also has access to a Ford Focus."

"Why would you wonder that?"

"I didn't want you to worry, but I think we're beyond that. The other night I was followed home by a tan Ford Focus."

"Are you sure it was really following you and not just going the same way?"

"Pretty sure. What's more is that I saw it again earlier tonight, parked outside of McNamara's on Lake."

"Did it follow you again?"

"No. Not that I could see."

"Maybe he knew a faster way to your house and beat you there... oh sorry. I didn't mean that as a pun."

"That's okay," Jack chuckled. "It was kind of funny."

Jack looked down at what he had written in his notebook. There were a couple of crossed out entries. Below these were the names *Percy Stuart* and *Mr. Dresden's Driver*. Jack realized that he had never been formally introduced to the man and therefore never learned his name. Next to this, he wrote the words *tan Ford Focus* He closed the notebook and stood up to place it back on his desk.

"Jack," Shelby began, "I think that I've gotten you in too deep." There was a pause before she continued. It took a lot for her to say her next words. "I want you to drop my case."

Jack set the notebook on the desk and turned around.

"I'm afraid I can't do that. Not now."

"Why not? You're going to get yourself killed."

"Because, like you just said. I'm in too deep and this guy who attacked me tonight already knows that I'm working this case. It's not like I can just call him up and say 'Forget it. I've dropped the case. You can stop trying to kill me now'." Jack was getting overly excited. "The only way he's going to stop is if I find out for certain who he is and put him away. Oh yeah, and there's no charge for any of this. At this point it's gotten personal."

"But Jack, you've already put so much into it. I should at least pay you something."

"Forget about it. And like you said to me the other night. You were so certain that I'm the one who finds him. Well, you're right. I will find him. One way or another I'll... find..."

Jack's head began to swim. The whole room felt as though it were moving around him. He went to put his left hand on his desk to steady himself, but suddenly felt the pain above his wrist from where he had been struck earlier. He recoiled his hand and lost his balance.

"Jack!"

Shelby quickly jumped up and ran across the room in an attempt to catch him but was just a moment too late. He dropped to his right knee and leaned against the desk.

"I'm okay," he assured her. "Just a little dizzy."

"My foot you are. You're laying back down."

She helped him up and escorted him across the room. When they got there, she helped him down onto the couch and knelt down on the floor beside him. Jack rested his head back on the pillows and closed his eyes for a few moments. When he opened them, he saw Shelby staring down at him with her bright blue eyes. She placed her right hand on his brow and slid it down the left side of his face. Jack felt as though he were caught in a dream. Nothing seemed quite real. Shelby gently placed her left hand on his shoulder, leaned forward and kissed his forehead. It was so light that it felt as though a feather was touching him. She pulled a few inches back, looked deep into his eyes, closed hers and placed her lips upon his. He tingled all over. He'd been kissed many times before, but never did it feel like this. It felt like magic. She slowly pulled her lips away so that only a miniscule amount of space separated them.

"I've wanted to do that for so long," she whispered.

"So have I," he quietly replied.

"Do you feel better?"

"Much. Thanks."

Shelby gently slid him over and crawled onto the couch beside him. He felt as if he were suddenly covered in a blanket of sheer comfort. She snuggled in closely to him and gazed into his eyes.

"I don't know what I'm feeling," she said, "but I don't think I've ever felt it before."

Jack wrapped his right arm around her and placed his hand upon her side.

"I don't think I have either. Not like this."

Shelby smiled at him and closed her eyes. Jack studied her face for a few minutes: the smoothness of her skin, the freckles on her nose, the melon hue of her lips. He smiled as he closed his eyes and drifted off to sleep with the calm, gentle feeling of Shelby Tomlinson's body pressed up against his.

Chapter 12

Jack awoke that bright Sunday morning to find that Shelby had left. Before she did though, she had covered him back up with the Indian blanket to keep him warm. He rubbed his eyes for a moment before looking around the room. He'd hoped that she would have left a note or something, but there was nothing to be found. He wondered when he would see her again.

It was just after ten o'clock. Every Sunday morning, Jack listened to the Irish Program on the AM radio. He walked over to his desk, tuned it in and heard the familiar brogue that he had woken up to so many times in the past. The host had been doing this program for many years now. Jack fondly remembered weekends that he'd spend as a child at his grandma and grandpa Martin's house in Parma. Each Sunday morning before church, his grandpa would be sitting at the kitchen table reading the newspaper while his grandma would be across the room burning the toast. Sitting on top of the refrigerator was an old transistor radio that religiously played this Irish program. Once in a while, Jack's grandpa would sing along to it, especially if it was playing the Clancy Brothers or Tommy Makem. Jack eventually picked up on some of the words and, as he grew older, would be sitting with his grandpa crooning along. This was how Jack came to learn so many Irish tunes.

After the first few songs were played and some birthday's and anniversaries announced, the host came back and started playing another tune: one by Jack's friend Ed from McNamara's. Though it had been played on there a few times before, he was still thrilled to hear his friend's music on the radio and hoped one day to hear his own. Then again, Whuppity Scoorie might have been considered a bit too rough for this show.

As the song ended, Jack heard his cell phone ring. His friends knew quite well not to bother him between ten and noon on Sundays. That was his time for listening to Irish music on the radio. Both of his grandparents had passed on many years earlier, quite prematurely actually, and this was his way of carrying on their tradition. Perhaps, he thought, it was Ed asking if he'd heard him on the radio. As Jack looked down at the caller ID, it turned out to be Corley, his downstairs neighbor. He considered letting it go to voicemail, but ultimately decided to answer it.

"Hello?" answered Jack.

"Hey, it's me," Corley replied.

"Morning, what's going on?"

"Hey, I'm down here on the front porch. Could you come down for a minute?"

Jack remembered the tussle last night. He had blacked out shortly afterward and could barely remember anything from it. He hoped that nothing was broken.

"Sure, I'll be down in a minute."

He hung up the phone, tightened the belt on his robe and walked down the stairs to the front door. There he found Corley waiting for him.

"What's up?" he asked Corley as he opened the door.

"Dude, what happened here? Oh my god! Your face!"

"Huh?" Jack looked down and saw a fair amount of blood on the porch. "Oh. It's a long story. I kind of got jumped last night."

"You're kidding me. Have you gone to the police?"

"Not yet. I'll take care of it later"

"I'll leave the blood here then, so that they can see it."

"No, that's okay. I'll clean it up in a bit."

"Don't you think we should at least take a picture to show them?"

"Don't bother."

"You're not going to do anything about it. Are you?"

"It's a little complicated," Jack explained.

"This has something to do with the new case that you're working. Doesn't it?" Jack gave her a funny look. He hadn't yet mentioned the new case to Corley. "I ran into Shaun yesterday afternoon when I went to Mac's to watch the Ohio State game. He told me that you were working a new case but that you wouldn't talk about it."

Jack considered it for a moment before he spoke. He was always square with Corley.

"Yeah. It has to do with the case."

"Damn, Jack. What the hell did you get yourself into?"

"Between you and me… it's a missing person's case. I'd

rather the others not know about it."

"You really need to call the cops."

"Went to them already, right to the sheriff's department. As far as they know, I've dropped this case."

"So why don't you?"

"Because I'm in too far to walk away. Besides, you know how I am when I get wrapped up in something."

"Yeah, it's called stubbornness," Corley informed him. Jack chuckled to himself a little, as he knew that she was right.

"What are you doing out here at this hour, anyway?" Jack asked. You usually sleep in on Sundays."

"Well, I saw the front porch light was burned out last night when I got home and figured I'd change it before I went out for the day."

"Burned out… I thought you turned it off again."

"Na, it's out. Oh, watch yourself when you're cleaning up that blood. There's some broken glass over there. You wouldn't know anything about that too. Would you?"

"What the hell?"

Jack crouched down and examined the small shattered pieces of glass that were lying about. He suddenly remembered his attacker taking a swing at him and missing and the cracking sound that accompanied this.

"I'll be back in a second," Corley told him. "I'm gonna get a stool and a new light bulb."

She walked back into her apartment leaving Jack on the porch by himself. He nervously looked about him as though he half-expected his attacker to come running out at him from the shrubs across the driveway. Realizing that this was absurd, he turned his attention back to the broken glass on the porch. There were a good dozen and a half pieces scattered about. He started to pick them up and set them down on the small drink table across the porch. He began to see an obvious pattern to the way they fit back together. Corley came back out after a moment and saw Jack putting broken glass on her table.

"Just don't leave those there," she said as she climbed on top of the stool and began to remove the light cover.

"Hey Corley, what does this look like to you?" Jack asked as he examined the broken glass. He'd fit them back together to form a perfect circle.

"Really?" Corley asked with astonishment.

"What?"

"Look!"

Jack looked up at the porch light and could see what Corley was agitated about. The light bulb wasn't burned out. It was missing.

"He must have been here earlier and removed it," Jack said with a realization. "Hey Corley, come here a minute."

Corley stepped down from the stool and walked over to Jack.

"What is it?"

"What does this look like?" he asked pointing down at the broken glass.

"I don't know. Bottom of a beer bottle? Some hippie broke his glasses? Some kind of lens, I guess."

"Yeah... a lens. Like from a flashlight."

Jack was back upstairs trying to catch the rest of his radio program. There was no longer any doubt in his mind that he had come face to face with Shelby's abductor the night before. He set down the shards of broken glass on his desk, rooted through the upper left-hand drawer for a moment and retrieved a roll of scotch tape. He began to pull off strips and hang them from the edge of his desk until he had accumulated a little less than ten of them. He then arranged the pieces of broken glass so that they once again formed a circle. Jack then placed the strips of tape across them so that the glass would hold its shape. So far, this was the closest thing that he had to a physical clue. Everything up until now had just been guesswork. Still, there was no way that he would be able to get anything even close to a fingerprint off of it.

After the Irish Program had concluded and the host had bid everyone a pleasant top o' the morning, Jack took a shower, dressed and drove up to the gas station to get a cup of coffee. It was now a quarter to one. He realized that he hadn't heard back from Maxine Rybarczyk about the property search that he'd requested. He had a pretty good idea about where the kidnapper had held the girls, but was pretty sure that this man hadn't lived there: especially if the house was condemned. He pulled out his

100

cell phone and gave Maxine a call, but there was no answer. He then remembered that it was Sunday and that if she would be anywhere, it'd be at an open house. Her firm was currently listing quite a few properties, but there was only one that she would be at and that was a two million dollar house in Bay Village. It was a sale that she was hoping to make quick work of.

Jack headed west on Lake Road until he came at last to the long driveway on the north side of the street. He pulled in, parked his car and stepped out. Usually, viewings for a home of this size and price range were by appointment only, but Maxine was hoping to generate a lot of buzz about it. She had definitely done that. There were fourteen other cars parked in the loop of the drive.

Jack found Maxine in the kitchen talking with a couple that had come to view the house.

"Well, here's a copy of the floor plan," she said as she handed them a slip of paper. "Feel free to browse around and if you have any questions, three more of my assistants are stationed throughout the house. They can tell you anything that you would want to know."

She looked up and saw Jack standing across the room.

"Jack," she said, slightly taken aback by the cuts on his face. "What happened to you?"

"Oh, it's nothing. Tripped going into my apartment."

"Busy night at Mac's?"

"Something like that."

"I'm sorry I still haven't gotten back to you with the information that you were seeking. It's been a busy weekend."

"I can tell," Jack replied as he looked about him. "This is quite a house."

"It'll be quite a commission too."

"No doubt there. You haven't gotten very far into that research yet, have you?"

"Not yet, but I'll have time on Monday."

"That's okay, I think I found the property I was looking for. It wasn't occupied by the man that I'm looking for, but I'm pretty sure that he'd used it."

"Where's it located?"

"Out in Greeley Township. The house that was there is long gone and it's now occupied by a housing development called

Fleur-de-lis Estates."

"I'm familiar with that property."

"You are?" Jack was a little astonished by this.

"Sure. There was a big push to save that house from the bulldozers."

"Why?"

"Well, it was quite a beautiful farmhouse back in its day. It was covered with gingerbread and had a pretty solid foundation. They even tried to have it added to the National Register of Historic Places, but it was torn down before the paperwork could be filed."

"Did it at least make it onto the Historic American Building Survey?"

"They didn't even get that far."

"You wouldn't happen to know any more about it, would you? Like who the original builder was?"

"I don't know the name of the family that it was built for, but if I remember correctly, the architect was a man named Grant Hollander. He usually designed prisons and reformatories. As far as I know, that was the only private residence that he had ever worked on. That's why there was such an effort to have it placed on the National Register of Historic Places."

"Prisons, huh?"

"Yeah, that's probably why it had such a strong foundation."

"Probably a pretty large basement, too."

"I'd imagine the cellar was quite vast. What are you thinking?"

Jack hadn't told Maxine about the details of the case, like how Shelby had been held in the basement of a house for fourteen days.

"I'm just wondering what more there is on this house."

"Well Jack, if anyone can find out more about a property, it's you."

While Jack was on his way back to Lakewood, he received a call from his cousin Trish, who had invited him up to My Friends on Detroit Avenue near West 117th Street for a late lunch. She was heading back down to Killington Hill that evening and wanted to have a chance to see him before she left. Although they exchanged emails regularly, it had been nearly three months since she had seen him and that was just for a few hours at the Martin family reunion. Jack thought it was a fluke that he should happen to call her a few days earlier and that she was already heading up that way. Trish knew there was more to this. Aside from all that, Pam would be joining them. She wanted to fill Jack in on what she'd done thus far.

Jack walked into the restaurant, passed the hostess' stand and took a seat at the table with his cousins.

"So how have you both been?" he asked.

"A lot better than you have, by the looks of it," Trish exclaimed. Jack got tired of explaining the cuts on the right side of his face.

"It's nothing."

"Like hell," she continued. "You found something. Didn't you?"

"Not exactly, but someone thinks I did."

"Was it our man?"

"I don't doubt it, but I didn't get a good look at him. It was dark and it happened rather quickly."

"You're lucky you weren't killed."

"I'm trying not to think about it," Jack said as though he wanted to change the subject. "So Pam, were you able to find anything out from the articles that I gave you yesterday?"

"Not yet, but the info on our Jane Does has been sent out to the places that you told me about. I should hear something back in a day or two. With luck, there will be a lead."

"I hope so. I only have two possible suspects and not much else to go on."

The waitress came over and took their orders. Both Trish and Pam ordered lunch, but Jack was just having a Pepsi. He didn't have much of an appetite at the moment.

"Did you hear, Trish?" Pam asked with a smile. "Jack handled a corpse yesterday."

"You're kidding me!" she replied, a look of shock on her face.

"Yeah, one of our pick-ups came in and Jack helped him

103

load it."

Jack dropped his head. He was happy this was amusing to at least someone.

"Getting over your fears?"

"Maybe a little," he told Trish as he looked over at Pam quite seriously. "By the way, never ask me to do that again."

"Oh come on, Jack," she said. "That was a once in a lifetime opportunity."

"Once in a lifetime?" he mused. "Glad to hear it."

"So?" began Trish, "Did you see her again last night?"

"Shelby?" Jack knew whom she meant.

"Of course, Shelby."

"Yeah. In fact, she helped me upstairs last night after I was attacked."

He paused for a moment, remembered the evening they had spent together and smiled.

"Something happened," Trish realized. "Didn't it?"

"Maybe."

"You know, Jack," she continued, "there's something about her. I don't know what it is, but I've never seen you like this."

"I know that I said I never get involved with clients, but… well… what a client."

"So when do we get to meet her?" Pam chimed in.

"I don't know. Soon, I hope. Things only really started to happen last night, but I guess she'd been feeling something for me for some time."

"And you?" Trish asked.

"Yeah, I've been thinking about her for a while too, I guess."

"Well good for you Jack," she continued. "It's about time you met someone."

They spent the next forty-five minutes at the restaurant talking about family and catching up on what everyone had been doing with their free time. Eventually, Jack excused himself, as he needed to get home. Trish figured it out that Shelby was likely coming over again. Jack wished her a safe drive back south and bid a good evening to both of them. He hoped Shelby was coming back that night.

Chapter 13

Jack fried up a steak in a skillet just after seven that evening. He served it up with sautéed mushrooms and onions and sat in front of the television as he ate. When he had finished, he rinsed his plate off and set it in the dishwasher. He walked back into the living room, stretched out on the couch and dozed off to sleep.

Occasionally, Jack would have dreams about the days that he had spent as a merchant marine, sailing on a freighter on the Great Lakes. These were usually anxiety dreams of some sort. They tended to be about missing the boat when he was supposed to be on board or about the ship going over Niagara Falls. Lately though, they'd been about the ship sinking. In some dreams, he was yelling at people to get below deck and in others he was racing to get out of his cabin before it flooded with water. The one he now had was of him trying to catch his breath as the last bit of air left his cabin. The next thing he knew, he was underwater.

Jack awoke suddenly from this nightmare around eight-thirty to see a beautiful set of bright blue eyes looking down at him.

"Bad dream?"

"Horrible." Jack caught his breath.

"I let myself in again," Shelby explained. Jack looked about the room. Apparently, she had also turned off the television.

"That's okay," he said as he sat up. "Feel free to do so any time."

"Actually, I'm a little surprised that the front door was unlocked; considering what had happened to you last night."

Jack thought about this. She was right. He had meant to lock the door once he'd returned home, but the idea had completely slipped his mind. He'd never had to lock his door before. He stood up at once and started for the stairs.

"I locked it behind me," Shelby continued. "I figured that it would be a good idea to do so."

Jack stopped halfway down, turned and came back up.

"Thanks. That just saved me a trip."

"So how was your day?" she asked as she took up a seat on

the couch.

"Not bad. A little on the busy side."

"How so?"

"Well, I found our first actual clue, but it's not going to do us much good."

Jack walked over to his desk, picked up the glass that he had taped together and handed it to Shelby.

"What's this?"

"It's the broken lens from a flashlight. Found it on the porch this morning. That's what I was beaten with last night."

"That's just like…"

"Yeah, I know, you and Lauren Call. Probably the others as well."

"So he has a weapon of choice?"

"It would appear so, but I doubt I'll ever get a fingerprint off of it. Especially since I handled each piece individually."

"Have you tried to find out what kind of flashlight it's from?"

Jack hadn't thought about that. He could have stopped at any number of stores that sold flashlights and made comparisons between them. Perhaps it was a specialty item: something that needed to be ordered directly from a company. This was unlikely, Jack thought. It'd be so much easier for anyone to just walk into any hardware store and buy a flashlight. Still, he thought that checking it out would be a good idea.

"I'll try to find out tomorrow," he told Shelby as he took a seat beside her.

"So what else happened today?"

"Well, I saw my cousins Pam and Trish."

"How are they?"

"Good. Trish was getting ready to drive back down to Killington Hill, so we met for lunch. Pam sent out the information on the Jane Doe cases that they have on file to the other cities that this guy has been in. She says she'll probably hear back in a couple of days."

"That's good. With luck, there will be something."

"Oh, I also met with my friend Maxine Rybarczyk earlier."

"Who's Maxine Rybarczyk?"

"She's a friend of mine that owns a realty company. I had

106

asked her a few days ago to do a search for me on real estate transactions from the general area that the kidnapper had struck back in the early nineties."

"Has she come up with anything?" Shelby was very interested in this approach that Jack had taken.

"Well, no. But I really don't think we need her to now."

"Why's that?"

"Because Trish has already figured out where you were taken."

"You mean the property in Greeley Township? I thought that was a dead end."

"I don't think so. Percy Stuart was one of two people that I talked to yesterday before I was attacked, which makes him a suspect. Also, Maxine told me a bit about the house that used to be there."

"What did she say?"

"Well, from what I understand, it was a house of some historical significance. Someone had tried to save it, but the house was ultimately demolished."

"Who tried to save it?"

"I don't know. I'm going to look into that tomorrow. To be honest though, I'm a little more interested in who demolished it. I think it may have been someone trying to hide evidence."

"That's a good thought," Shelby told him. "Do you really think that's where I was taken?"

"I'm fairly certain. Maxine said that the architect mainly designed prisons. That sounds like the perfect place to hold someone. I'd imagine that the basement walls were quite thick and that it'd be nearly impossible for anyone to hear anything coming from in there. I'm going to see what more I can find out on it tomorrow."

"Sounds like you have a busy day ahead of you," Shelby said with a smile.

"I always have a busy day ahead of me. It's funny too. I always thought that going the route of self-employment meant that I'd get to sleep in on some days. Guess I was wrong."

There was a long pause from Shelby. It almost looked as if she was uneasy about something. Jack figured that it had something to do with the connection they made to one another the night before. She had seemed a little standoffish since arriving and this worried him. Finally, she spoke up.

"Look, Jack, about last night..." she began. Here it was. Jack had heard this too many times before. It was the whole 'I made a mistake' speech.

"It's okay," he interrupted. "You're my client and we shouldn't be involved. You don't have to explain..."

"No, Jack, that's not where I was going with this."

"You weren't?"

"No. I want to tell you that I'm really sorry about what happened to you last night and that if you want to drop this case, it'll be okay with me. I don't want you to get hurt again."

"Oh."

"Do you think we shouldn't get involved?"

"No," he said abruptly. "Usually I'd say yes, but I can't deny that I've developed feelings for you. I just thought that's what you were going to say."

"I wasn't going to say that, Jack. I have feelings for you too. What surprises me is that I managed to go this long without saying or doing anything about it."

"You know what's funny? We hardly know anything about each other."

"I like that. It keeps some of ze mystery between us," Shelby said with a bad Russian accent and her eyebrows furrowed. Jack liked her sense of humor. "Besides," she said as she relaxed her expression, "we'll have plenty of opportunities to learn more about each other as time goes on."

"Still, it'd be nice to know something about you."

"Okay, what do you want to know?"

Jack wasn't actually prepared to ask her anything and jumped at the first thought that entered his mind.

"Well, where did you go to school?"

"School? Um... I attended B.W. and graduated in 99' with a degree in veterinary medicine."

"B.W.? You're joking me. That's where I got my degree in history."

"Really?" she said, slightly astonished. "Small world."

"Small town; Cleveland I mean, not Berea; which obviously is. So what do you do now?"

108

"I work with animals. I'm a vet. It was always my dream to become one. It took a while, but I finally made it happen. Anything else?"

"Sure. What's your phone number?"

"That's a secret. You'll get it eventually though."

She placed her hands on his shoulders and glanced at the cuts on the side of his face. "These seem to be healing nicely. And to think that all of that blood came from just a few little scrapes."

"I can hardly even feel it."

"How's the wrist?"

"A little bruised and stiff, but otherwise it's fine."

"That's good," she said softly as she gazed into his eyes. She drew herself in closely and again, they were kissing each other. Jack lost himself in a haze. He couldn't figure out what it was about her that made him feel so calm. It was like being intoxicated, yet he hadn't touched a drop all day. It was pure euphoria being in her arms. He lost all touch with where reality ended and dreaming began.

The next thing Jack knew, it was two in the morning. Three lit candles were sitting on his coffee table, flickering an amber glow upon the walls. His head was resting on a large pile of pillows and he was covered with a large blanket from his bedroom. Shelby was gone again.

Chapter 14

Jack awoke that Monday morning to find the sun streaming in through his bedroom window and casting its light upon his face. He had crawled into bed the night before just after he'd realized that Shelby had left. He didn't even bother to change into his sweatpants. Despite the fact that he was only dressed in his boxers, he felt unusually warm. He threw the blanket off and walked over to the window. He opened it to find a beautifully warm day. Indian summer had finally arrived.

There was much to do that day. He knew this and didn't want to waste any time in getting started. He turned on the television to briefly catch the headlines on the morning news. The first five stories were pretty boring, but weatherman promised that the fine temperatures would hang around for at least the next two days. The next story was about a groundbreaking for a new office park on the east side: again, boring to Jack.

He clicked off the television and walked directly into the bathroom to shave and take a shower. Lately, he'd have to crank the hot water on high, but that morning, it didn't seem quite as necessary. As he lathered his hair with shampoo, he tried to put his plans for the day in order, but found that he was getting distracted. It was going to be a beautiful day. If he weren't so busy, he'd have called his friend Ryan and would have attempted to get him to play hooky from work to go rock climbing at Virginia Kendall Ledges in Peninsula. This was out of the question. He had an obligation to Shelby and knew that time was running out for Rebecca Lowe. If he could find the man that had attacked him on Saturday night, he knew that he'd find the missing girl.

Jack dried himself off and tossed on a pair of jeans and his Ghoulardi tee shirt. He threw on his most comfortable pair of Doc Martins, as he knew there was going to be a lot of footwork that day. It would all have to start at home though. He walked over to his desk, turned on his laptop and pulled out his notebook. The computer booted up and within a couple of minutes, he was surfing the net. He would have to learn more about the old house in Greeley Township before he could proceed any further.

He started with the Cuyahoga County Recorder's website.

The earliest he had been able to find thus far was an owner named Archibald A. Swift. He'd have to start there and see how far back he could go. Jack entered Mr. Swift's name and soon found that the man had owned that property since the early nineteen fifties. The previous owner was a woman named Gertrude M. Vaule. After checking the Cleveland Necrology File, he learned that her husband, Robert, had passed away in 1949 and that she had inherited the property from him. The obituary went on to give a late address of 4021 Indianola Road. Jack made a note of this, as he was certain that it would be of use to him later. He next returned to the county recorder's website and entered the name *Robert Vaule*. He found that Mr. Vaule had purchased that property in 1910. There were three sellers names listed in this transaction. All had the last name of Rainey. Jack went back to the necrology page and typed in *Rainey*. He scanned the obituary abstracts until he found what he was looking for.

Name: *Rainey, Frank R.*
Date: *August 7, 1909*
Source: *Cleveland Press; Cleveland Necrology File, Reel #067*
Notes: *Rainey, Frank, beloved husband of the late Mary. Father of Joseph, Christian and Frank Jr. In his 72nd year. Friend received at one O'clock Tuesday at late residence on Indianola Road, Greeley Township. Please omit flowers. Burial private.*

The names Joseph, Christian and Frank matched up with the names of the sellers to Mr. Vaule. Jack quickly went back to the recorders website, typed in *Frank R. Rainey* and found what he was looking for. Mr. Rainey, as it turned out, had purchased the property in 1865. Back then, the property was considerably larger. Jack noticed that over the course of the next six years, Mr. Rainey had sold off a few acres. He looked at whom he had purchased it from and came up with the name Perkins. Jack had come across that name in his research many times before. The Perkins' were big landowners back in their day. It was unlikely that any of them had actually lived on that land, which would make Mr. Rainey the original owner of the house. Jack had his starting point. He turned off the laptop and was ready to begin his running around.

As he stood up, he placed his wallet in his back pocket, cell phone in his front, grabbed his keys and notebook, scratched Fionn's ears for a second and was out the door. As he descended the front steps, he suddenly stopped cold and took a look about him. For a moment, he thought he was going to be attacked by someone who had been laying in wait outside of his apartment all night. As it was though, the coast was clear. The only form of life that Jack could see on his street was a couple of black squirrels chasing each other around a tree trunk. He hopped into his car and drove off.

Jack walked up the steps of the Cuyahoga County Archives building and entered through the front door. He checked the time, signed in and placed his notebook on a table in the side room. He had visited this office many times in the past, usually doing property research for Maxine or looking up death and marriage records for genealogy projects. The county archives office was housed in the old Robert Russell Rhodes house on Franklin Boulevard. It was a red brick building of Italianate design and was built sometime during the later half of the nineteenth century. Back then, Franklin was considered Cleveland's millionaires row. This, of course, was before Euclid Avenue saw its heyday. The Rockefellers had moved out there and the big money was soon to follow. The fact was that Franklin once had many mansions like the Rhodes house. Sadly, most of these were long gone.

Jack browsed the many books along the shelf and searched through the different subjects: prominent people, veterans, abstracts and cemeteries. He finally found what he wanted. There were many titles among the section on townships, but only one book about Greeley. He pulled it off the shelf and took it over to the table where he opened it to the index and scanned the column until he found the name *Rainey, Frank... page 220*. After flipping to page 220, he located a mention of Mr. Rainey and read on.

There wasn't much of interest to him in this tome. All that it said was that Frank Rainey had come to Greeley Township in 1863 from Albany, New York. He had enlisted with the Union Army at the onset of the American Civil War in 1861 and had served for 120 days, after which he had traveled to Ohio with his wife, Mary, and two-year-old son, Joseph. It went on to say that he was a prominent farmer and blacksmith. There was no picture of him or of his house.

Jack had only just broken the surface on this. As he placed the book back on the shelf, Ellen, the head archivist entered the room.

"How are you doing today, Jack," she asked with a smile.

"Not bad. Just looking up a few things."

"What happened to your face?"

"Oh, its nothing. Took a spill on my bike." Jack didn't even own a bike, but Ellen didn't know this. He just didn't feel like telling her about what had happened and saw no harm in a little light lie such as this.

"Well, whatever happened to you," she continued, "you have that look in your eye again and I can tell you're onto something big. What's the project?"

"Just a house out in Greeley Township. They tore it down a few years ago."

"Haunted?" Ellen was quite familiar with the usual field of Jack's research.

"I don't think so. Designed by a prominent architect though. Someone named Hollander, I think."

"Grant Hollander? I thought he only did prisons." Ellen was something of an authority on local architects. If there was anyone who could tell him more about Hollander, she certainly could.

"So you've heard of him?"

"I'm surprised that you haven't," she replied. "He was quite a prolific architect in his day. Back then they were designing prisons to look as scary as humanly possible. It was a hope that the very appearance of an institution would scare a criminal into a life of the straight and narrow. Hollander took this a few steps further. He would ornament the entrances to his structures with images of demons and other monsters carved out of stone. I didn't know that he had ever done any houses though."

"From what Maxine has told me, he had."

"That must have been some house then. I wouldn't mind seeing a picture of it."

"I'm hoping to find one myself. That's one of the reasons that I dropped by."

"Do you have an address or a Permanent Parcel Number?"

"I have an address." Jack opened up his notebook. "It's 4021 Indianola Road."

"Well, let me see what we have."

Ellen jotted down the address on a slip of paper and walked out of the room. She had gone to retrieve a county property card. Back in the 1960's, the Cuyahoga County Auditor's Office had done a property assessment on every tax-assessed property in the county. Over the years though, many of these had gone missing. Still, it was worth a look. A moment later, Ellen had returned with a card in her hand.

"This is all we have. No picture I'm afraid."

She handed the card to Jack who sat down and looked it over. The information was pretty vague. It gave the dimensions of the house and property along with the owner's name of Archibald A. Swift. Jack could see where there had once been a picture pasted in the upper left hand corner. A small and dried out dab of glue was all that remained.

"Doesn't really tell me that much," Jack noted. "It does say that it was a stone house with a slate roof and that it was built in 1885."

"I don't think that's right though," Ellen said.

"How do you mean?"

"Well, Grant Hollander died in 1881, so either the date listed is incorrect or it wasn't designed by Hollander."

"Can I check the tax records?"

"Sure, Jack. You know where they are."

Jack picked up his notebook and proceeded to walk down the long corridor that took him into the back of the building. Many rooms came off of this hallway. Each contained some collection of different documents. Jack thought that the rooms reminded him of the classrooms at the catholic school he had once attended: cold tile floors and poorly lit. He entered the last room on his right and immediately set himself to locating the tax book for Greeley Township starting with 1865: the year that Frank Rainey had first purchased that property.

The book listed Mr. Rainey as owning 74 acres at a value of seven thousand dollars. Jack pulled the books for the years that followed. He noticed that with each year until 1872, the property size diminished slightly. Eventually, it settled at 41 acres and a value of five thousand dollars. Then, in 1876, the value jumped by ten thousand dollars, yet the size of the land remained the same. That had to be it. That had to be the year that Frank Rainey contracted Grant Hollander to design his house. Jack made his notes and returned the tax book to its proper place. As he did so, he heard a man's voice from right behind him.

"Greeley Township tax records, eh? Not much of interest out there."

Jack nearly jumped out of his skin. As near as he knew, the room was empty. He turned to see a man in his mid-forties standing behind him and leaning up against a bookshelf. He was quite taken aback by the sudden appearance of this man. He had long graying hair, a gray goatee, fierce looking eyes with crow's feet and heavy eyebrows. He was also dressed in a brown duster and looked to be quite eccentric.

"I'm sorry if I startled you," the stranger continued. "Actually, I was just coming in to look at that same book."

Jack glanced over at the shelf where he had just placed the tax book for Greeley Township.

"I was just finishing up with it," Jack told him.

"And did you find anything interesting?"

"It's a tax record. How interesting can that be?"

The stranger nodded with a smile as he walked passed Jack and reached for the dust covered volume.

"Good point. Still," he said as he opened the large book, "You can find out so much from these. They're really a record of those who came before us. For instance, look at this guy." He pointed at a page that had the name *Lescher* written on it. "Mr. Lescher here owned well over a hundred acres. Now I wonder why."

"He must have been a farmer," Jack concluded.

"Maybe, but not at land values like this. By the looks of it, I'd say this land was mostly wooded. Perhaps he was an avid hunter or just liked to keep the land as he had first found it. Oh, I'm sorry. Where are my manners? Orin Drury." The man introduced himself as he balanced the open book in his left hand and extended his right. Jack shook it and likewise introduced himself.

"Jack Sullivan."

"No, wait, let me guess. John Martin Sullivan, the author?"

"Yeah," Jack said with a smile. "But how did you…"

"Know who you were? Your picture is on the back of your books."

"Oh," Jack chuckled.

"So what's so important in Greeley Township that the celebrated historian is looking up today?"

Jack shot him an odd look. He was right in guessing that this man was something of an eccentric. Nonetheless, he saw no harm in sharing his research with Mr. Drury. That and he was beginning to like the curious stranger.

"It's a house out on Indianola Road that was torn down a few years back. I'm trying to learn more about it for a client."

"That would be the Rainey House if I'm not mistaken, and I rarely am."

"That's right, the Rainey House. But…"

"How did I know?" Orin Drury interrupted again. "Well, it's the only house of note in that area that has been torn down in recent years. Built by Hollander in 1876, as I'm guessing you've just learned."

"That's incredible. Are you an architectural historian?"

"No. I'm an archivist."

"Really? I've not seen you here before."

Mr. Drury leaned in closer to Jack and spoke in little more than a whisper.

"There are other archives in this city besides this one."

"Of course," Jack replied. "There are many libraries…"

"No, no, no! That would make me a librarian, which I am not. I am an archivist."

"Okay," Jack said slightly startled by the man's change in demeanor. "So which archives do you work for?"

"I work for no archives," Orin Drury calmly said with a smile. "The archives work for me. It's a private collection."

"I see." Jack was really beginning to like this guy, but found him odder and odder with each passing moment.

"No, you don't see, but I wouldn't mind if you did."

At this, Orin Drury seemed to produce a business card out of thin air and handed it to Jack.

116

"Carter's Closet: antiques, vintage and so much more," Jack read aloud.

"It's the 'so much more' aspect that I think you'd be interested in more than anything else, Mr. Sullivan."

"Oh, you'd be surprised. I have quite a collection of antiques. And it's Jack."

"Very well, Jack. Feel free to drop by anytime you wish."

"Thank you Mr. Drury. Wait a minute. You wouldn't happen to be related to the Drury's of Euclid Avenue by chance, would you?"

"Once upon a time and in another life I was. And if you're Jack, then I'm Orin."

"Thanks Orin. It was nice meeting you. I'll be sure to stop by and check out your store."

"Please do. I'm certain that you won't be disappointed. And good luck with your research."

"Thanks," Jack said as he exited the room. He had the distinct feeling that he had just met some kind of a magician.

"Did you find it then?" Ellen asked Jack as he reemerged from the back rooms.

"According to the tax record, it was built in 1876."

"So it could have been a Hollander house."

"I'm pretty sure it was," Jack said thinking back on all that Orin Drury knew about the property. "I think I'm going to hit up the library to see if I can find a photo."

Jack walked over to the register, looked up at the clock and signed out.

"Good luck, Jack," Ellen said as he started for the door. "Don't forget, I want to see a picture of that house."

After circling the block a few times, Jack had finally found a spot at a one-hour parking meter. He would either have to be quick with his research, here at the Cleveland Public Library's Main Branch, or make multiple trips to the meter. This library was an amazing source of information, but the parking was atrocious. Twice in the past, Jack had received tickets for having his meter expire. In one case, he had walked up to his car while the meter cop was waiting. As he opened his door, the meter expired and the attendant printed the ticket. According to this attendant, it didn't matter that he was at his vehicle. The meter had expired and the vehicle was still parked there.

Jack entered the new Louis Stokes Wing and took the elevator up to the fourth floor. It was here that the photograph collection was housed. Normally, he would have had to make a request for a photograph by title, but recently, photographs of houses had been scanned into a computer, where it would be viewable with just a few clicks of a button. Jack entered the keyword *Indianola* and began to browse through the many images that came up. A moment later, he was looking upon the image of a brooding stone house with gargoyles that flanked the front gate. Here it was: 4021 Indianola Road.

After writing down the photo code number, Jack handed it to the librarian who went to retrieve the original from the files. He handed Jack a pair of white cotton document gloves that were way too small to fit his hands. Still, Jack put them on as best he could, took the photograph to the copier and made a duplicate. After handing back the original, the librarian stamped the photocopy and Jack was off. As he rode the elevator back down to the main floor, he took a long look at the photo. The house was immense. It stood three stories high and was ornamented with gingerbread trim and what looked to be iron spikes running along the peak. Had this house been located somewhere along the lake, Jack would have thought this to be a widow's walk. As it was though, the house was pretty far inland and didn't have mansard walls or a flat roof. The spikes were purely ornamental. It was a shame, Jack thought, that this house had been razed. It was quite a beautiful structure.

Jack exited the elevator and walked out of the library onto Superior Avenue. He rounded the corner and headed north up East Sixth Street until he came to his car. There were still two minutes remaining on his meter and he could see the attendant making his way up the street. Jack jumped into the car and drove off. He'd won this round, but was certain that until the parking situation improved downtown, there would be more tickets in his future.

As he made his way back towards the West Side, Jack briefly considered stopping back at the archives office to give Ellen a copy of the picture that he had just located. Unfortunately, there was still much to do. He'd have to drop it off another time.

He continued back to his house to look up more information online. He realized that he should have done this earlier, but the thought had slipped his mind. It now meant making another stop.

He raced up the stairs and booted up his laptop. He returned to the Cleveland News Index and typed in the keyword *Swift*. All that it brought up was a series of obituary entries. He tried a different approach and entered the name *Rainey*. Again, it was more obituaries, but among them was an entry that read *Rainey House Is No More*. The Cleveland News Index, aside from obituaries, also listed a few headlines. Jack wrote down the corresponding date, section and page and was off once again. This time he made his way out to Fairview Park. He'd used the library there many times before, mainly for its genealogy resources, but also because they didn't charge for copies.

It was starting to get later in the afternoon and Jack was starting to get a bit antsy. He was still hoping to enjoy part of the day outside, perhaps by taking lunch up at Lakewood Park. This would have to wait.

He entered the library and strode up the stairs to the second floor. It was here that Cleveland newspapers from the past were stored on microfilm. Jack set his notebook down beside a microfilm viewer, walked over to a drawer and pulled out a reel of film marked as being The Plain Dealer from early March of 1995. He returned to the viewer, loaded the film and began to scan the pages. After a moment, he found the article.

Rainey House Is No More
119-year-old Victorian house demolished

The 119-year-old farmhouse that has stood at 4021 Indianola Road in Greeley Township has met its fate. Despite all efforts to save the aged structure from the wrecking ball, the historic house came crashing down yesterday afternoon. The property has been at the center of much debate over the past few months with the Greeley Historical Society making a push to preserve the home. There had been talk of intervention from the Federal Government to step in, by placing the house on the

119

National Register of Historic Places, but those efforts never came to fruition.

Denise DeLang, president of the GHS, has expressed the tragic feeling felt throughout the community at the loss of this house. "It really is a shame that we should lose such an asset to our neighborhood. Houses such as this are becoming more and more rare."

Percy Stuart, the owner of the property, could not be reached for comment. Mr. Stuart, president of Stuart Shipping and Handling, had originally planned to turn the site into a shipping hub, but the Greeley Township Zoning Board of Directors had turned him down for a variance. Following his final appeal, Mr. Stuart expressed interest in selling the property. His decision to demolish the house remains a mystery to Mrs. DeLang and many others.

"Why tear down such a beautiful home if you have no intention of using the land? Why not sell it to someone who would be interested in restoring it?"

The house, considered a true showpiece of the area, was built in the mid-1870's for a prominent farmer named Frank Rainey, who occupied it until his death in 1909. It then passed through a series of owners until being purchased by Mr. Stuart in 1990. It has been considered structurally unsafe for many years and was condemned in 1993.

Jack had his answers. He had originally thought that the house had been torn down to make way for the housing development that now occupied the site, but this turned out to be false. It was Percy Stuart that had ordered the demolition of the house, and without any apparent good reason. Perhaps, Jack thought, he was trying to hide something. He quickly printed out the article and placed it in his notebook next to the picture of the house that he had found earlier.

Aside from all of this, Jack had also learned whom it was that had tried to save the house. Granted, it was quite a few years back, but perhaps Denise DeLang at the Greeley Historical Society could shed some more light on this story. Jack walked over to the short reference section and located a phone book. He quickly found a listing for the GHS, wrote down the number and collected his notebook. A moment later, he was in his car and heading back towards Lakewood.

Jack pulled out his cell phone and the number for the GHS. He dialed and soon was speaking with an elderly woman.

"Good afternoon," he began. "My name is John Sullivan and I'm trying to locate someone named Denise DeLang."

"I'm sorry," the woman replied, "but Mrs. DeLang passed away a little over a year ago."

"Oh, I'm sorry."

"That's alright. My name is Sheila. Is there anything that I can help you with?"

"Perhaps. I'm calling in regards to a house that your group had made an effort to save a few years back."

"That wouldn't happen to be the Rainey House, would it?"

"It is."

"Ah, that was such a treasure to all of us. It broke Denise's heart when they tore it down."

"Well, I was wondering if you could tell me a little more about it."

"Certainly. What would you like to know?"

"Well, I'm curious about the circumstances surrounding its demolition. I recently came across an article about it, but it said that Percy Stuart couldn't be reached for comment. Did anyone ever confront him on the matter afterward?"

"Yes. It took a while, but Denise finally got through."

"What did he have to say?"

"Well, he told her that by removing the house, the property would have been easier to sell."

"Did she believe him?"

"Not for one second. There were plenty of interested parties in the area that would have been more than happy to purchase that property just as it was: Denise and her husband Mick included."

"Why didn't he sell it to them?"

"No one knows. She had made him an offer and he said that he'd consider it. The next thing we knew, it was being knocked down."

"And he sold the property about a year later. There's now a housing development there."

"I know. It's not like we need any more of those around. Damned cookie-cutter houses. They all look the same."

"Had you ever been inside of the house?"

"Once, when we were surveying the property."

"What do you remember about it?"

"Oh, it was a beauty. Had really large rooms with high ceilings and very ornamental woodwork throughout."

"Did you ever see the basement?"

"The basement? Yeah, we took a walk down there. It had really thick stone walls. Sort of reminded me of being in a jail."

"Well, I guess that's about all I can think of."

"I hope I was able to be of some help, Mr. Sullivan."

"Thank you. You really have been. You have a good day now."

"And you. Thank you."

Jack ended his call. Percy Stuart looked a lot like his prime suspect.

Chapter 15

On his way back to Lakewood, Jack made a brief stop at the hardware store two blocks from his street. He was interested in what kind of flashlight he had been struck with on Saturday night. He entered the store, walked over to an isle that held a wide variety of flashlights and pulled the reassembled lens from his pocket. He made his way down the isle holding it up to every one that he came to. In no time, he had found a match. It was from a Mag-Lite, and a large one at that. Unfortunately, it was also quite common. It could have been picked up anywhere and by anyone. This wasn't much of a clue after all. The only connection between it and the kidnapper was that it seemed to be his weapon of choice.

As he approached his house, Jack could see that he had company. Much to his astonishment, the tan Ford Focus was parked in his driveway. This was a bold move for his attacker, to sit and wait for him in his own driveway in broad daylight. He was half tempted to keep driving. Part of him was screaming to call the police while the rest of him said to deal with it himself. With his heart pounding, he parked his car up the street and decided to act on his latter impulse. He stepped out of the Mazda Protegé 5, popped the hatchback and retrieved the tire iron. With much deliberate intent, he walked back down the street towards his house brandishing his makeshift weapon.

"Out!" he shouted as he approached. "Get out of the car!" He raised the tire iron into the air. The door flung open and he was standing face to face with a man in his late thirties wearing a black suit and a tie. This didn't make sense. He was too young to be Percy Stuart and he certainly wasn't Mr. Dresden's driver. As Jack drew nearer, he caught a glimpse of the license plate. It read *U.S. Government*, contained a few numbers and letters and at the bottom were the words *for official use only*. The man quickly held out a badge and introduced himself.

"Mr. Sullivan. I'm Special Agent Andrew Spurlock of the Federal Bureau of Investigation." He had his right hand hidden inside of his jacket. Jack could only assume that it was resting on the butt of a gun. "If you'll be so kind as to lower your weapon."

Jack immediately placed the tire iron on the ground and

slowly raised his hands into the air.

"It's alright, Mr. Sullivan. You can put your hands down." Jack obeyed.

"Are you the one who's been following me?"

The federal agent removed his hand from inside his jacket.

"I must apologize for that," the agent said. "I was acting on a tip and had to follow protocol."

"How long have you been following me?"

"Since Thursday evening, but it hasn't been every night."

"I see."

"Would it be alright if we spoke together somewhere a bit more private than this?"

Jack glanced at his door.

"Sure. Come on up. Would it be okay if I didn't leave this here?" Jack asked, motioning at the tire iron he had set on the ground.

"That would be fine. After you."

Jack unlocked his front door and escorted the agent up the stairs and into his apartment. He set the tire iron on the floor and offered his guest a seat on the couch.

"So you've been following me on and off for the past few days. Why?"

"Well, like I said, we received a tip and had to follow up on it."

"What sort of a tip?"

"The kind that comes from the Cuyahoga County Sheriff's Department."

"Ah."

"After you had met with Sheriff's Deputy Edward Lauber, our bureau was contacted and from what he had told us, there seemed to be some merit to what you were looking into."

"So you believe these cases are connected as well?"

"I didn't say that. I simply said that there seemed to be some merit."

"And who decides that?"

"My orders to follow up on a lead come directly from the special-agent-in-charge of the FBI office here in Cleveland."

"Do you think there's some merit?"

"I've looked into it some and believe that you may have

stumbled onto something. Speaking of which, you didn't have those cuts on your face when I saw you Saturday night. Do you mind telling me what happened?"

"I don't mind telling you at all. In fact, it'd have been nice if you had followed me home on Saturday night. I was jumped outside of my place here, sometime just before eleven."

"Did you get a good look at your assailant?"

"No. He'd been here earlier and had removed the light bulb from my front porch. I thought about going to the police, but the sheriff's department already made it clear that they didn't want me on this case. I didn't want word getting to them that I was still on it."

"You really should have gone to the police. We'd have been having this conversation a lot sooner than this."

"Well, its not like there was any real evidence to go on. The guy hit me with a flashlight a few times. All I could find was this. It's not like you could get fingerprints from it"

Jack retrieved the shattered flashlight lens from his pocket and handed it to the agent.

"Have you searched for the light bulb?"

"Honestly? No. Hell, for all I know, he took it with him."

"Or tossed it somewhere. I'll check the shrubs when I leave."

Jack was a little disappointed that he hadn't thought to do this.

"Here's a question." Jack interjected. "If the sheriff's department has a suspect in custody, why is any of what I'm looking into of any interest to the bureau?"

"You haven't seen the news today, Mr. Sullivan. Have you?"

"No. Why?"

"Their suspect was released early this morning. There wasn't enough evidence to charge him, let alone hold him for questioning any further."

"Really?" Jack was astonished that he'd missed this. Had he not been in such a hurry to leave the house that morning, he'd have caught the news and would have seen the story of the suspect's release.

"What I'd like to start off by knowing is why you seem to

think that the disappearance of Rebecca Lowe is connected with some missing persons cases from the early nineties."

"Well, look at the facts. For one, it's the same area. The girl matches the age and ethnicity of the priors. There was blood found on the ground in the vicinity of where she went missing. It was the same with the others, and these as well."

Jack walked over to his desk and pulled out the files that Shelby had given him on the missing girls from the other states. He handed them to the federal agent who slowly leafed through them. The agent pulled out a small notepad and began to scribble down a few notes. After a couple of minutes, he set the files down on the coffee table and looked at Jack.

"And you don't think it could be a copycat?"

"In five different states? Not at all. This person would have had to do some extensive research. They would have also had to interview Lauren Call, and from what I was told, she hasn't spoken of what had happened to her in years." Jack decided against mentioning Shelby to the federal agent. The anonymity of his clients was golden. That and he didn't want to bring her into all of this.

"You spoke with Lauren Call?"

"That's right. A few days ago. She told me that there were inaccuracies in what the newspapers had printed versus what had actually happened to her. From what I've been able to find, their scenarios seem to match up pretty closely. Oh, there's also the fact that someone attacked me on Saturday night. Apparently someone thinks that I may have stumbled onto something."

"So you have suspects?"

"Now that you mention it, I do. Two, in fact. The only two that I had mentioned this case to that seem to fit the bill."

"And who would these suspects be?"

"Well, one is the driver of a past client. I don't know his name, but he's the personal chauffeur of Claude Dresden of Chagrin Falls."

"Why do you suspect him?"

"For starters, I had mentioned the case to him earlier on Saturday afternoon. Also, he's a chauffeur. Lauren Call told me that her attacker was dressed as one. There was also the smell."

"What smell is that?"

126

"The chemical smell," Jack explained. "Lauren said that there was a strong chemical smell that accompanied her attacker. On Saturday, I saw him dumping something called Witch Hazel on his hands. The smell was horrible."

"I'm familiar with Witch Hazel, as well as the smell. It's an astringent used for skin irritations."

"That's what he said it was for."

"Alright, we'll keep him in mind." The agent made a note of this. "Who was your other suspect?"

"Percy Stuart."

"Okay. Who's Percy Stuart?"

"He used to own a property out in Greeley Township."

"And that relates to this case how?"

"Well, I have reason to believe that this kidnapper took these girls out to that property."

"Why would you think that?"

"If it's all the same, I'd rather not say at this time. But there used to be an old house on the site. It was designed by a man named Hollander, who was famous for building prisons. This guy Percy Stuart owned it during the first half of the nineties. Then, for no good reason at all, decided to tear the place down. I think he was trying to hide something out there. I also spoke to him on Saturday."

"Alright then, Mr. Sullivan," the agent said as he made a final note, "I'll look into these two suspects that you have and see where they were on Saturday evening." He reached into his wallet, retrieved a small business card and handed it to Jack. "Here's my card. If you have any more thoughts or trouble, feel free to call me. My cell phone number's on the back."

Jack took the card and looked it over.

"Thanks," he said as he placed it on his desk.

"As far as the sheriff's department goes, I wouldn't worry about what you were told. I can't ask you to keep looking into this and I can't condone what you've done so far. You seem to be doing a good job of it, though. If you do decide to continue your investigation, I'd prefer it if you wouldn't mention this case to anyone else or make any more phone calls in regards to it."

"That seriously limits me."

"Look, I know there's something more here that you're not

telling me, like how you came up with a property in Greeley Township. You've shared with me, so I'll share a bit with you. We were looking into that area back in the early nineties. It did seem to fit as a central area to where this kidnapper was striking. We never did find anything though. When the disappearances stopped occurring, the trail went cold and the cases were eventually buried."

Jack knew that this meant that he was on the right track.

"I really appreciate you taking the time to talk with me Agent Spurlock. You're not going to be following me anymore, are you?"

"No," he replied, "but I will ask the Lakewood police to step up patrols in this area after dark."

"That's greatly appreciated. I'm sure my downstairs neighbor will be happy to hear it."

As the evening wore on, Jack spent much of the time on his computer doing some follow-up work for his mother on the Martin family tree. He had his windows open, as it was turning out to be a beautiful evening. He hadn't made it up to the park for lunch as he had hoped and ended up settling on a bowl of ramen noodle soup and a couple of grilled cheese sandwiches for dinner. It was getting dark earlier and earlier and he couldn't help but wonder how much longer it would be before Shelby came over.

After a bit, an email came in from an acquaintance in Iowa. He'd been waiting to hear back from this person for a few days now, as it was in regards to a cursed rag doll, an item that he'd been trying to locate for quite some time now. The email explained that the doll had been sold during the early 1920's to a man named Cyrus Winston that operated a carnival. After that, there was no further record. This meant that Jack would have to do some serious looking into who Mr. Winston was and if he had any children. Perhaps some of them might still be alive and know what became of the doll.

He started to look up Cyrus Winston's name on a genealogical website, but heard his doorbell ring. He quickly descended the stairs and opened the door at the bottom. Peering down the next set of stairs, he could see Shelby looking back up at him from outside the front door. He raced to the bottom and let her in.

"So you figured out which doorbell was mine?" he asked.

"Yeah, it wasn't that hard really: third floor, third from the left. Worst case scenario, I get the wrong apartment."

"Good point. Come on up."

Jack let her in and closed the door behind her.

"It's good to see that you're locking your door now," she added.

"I meant to the other night, but it had slipped my mind to do so."

They entered the apartment and Jack offered her a seat on the couch. Before she sat, she gave him a quick peck on the cheek. He lost his train of thought for a moment, but quickly regained his composure and took a seat next to her.

"I had an interesting conversation today," he began.

"Oh? Who with?"

"Special Agent Andrew Spurlock of the FBI."

"Really? What did he want?"

"Well, apparently he was tipped off that I was looking into the disappearance of Rebecca Lowe as well as some other missing girl's cases from the early nineties. This piqued the bureau's interest and they had him follow me on and off for the last few evenings."

"The man in the Focus?"

"That's him."

"So what did he tell you?"

"Not much really. Asked questions more than anything else."

"Like what?"

"Like why I thought the Lowe girl's disappearance was related to the others."

"Did you tell him?"

"Of course I told him. I also told him who my suspects were. There's only two, so it shouldn't be long before he figures out which one it is."

"What about you, though?"

"What about me?"

"Are you still going to be looking into this?"

"Well," Jack paused and thought for a moment before

129

continuing, "he didn't tell me to stop, so yes, I guess I'll still be looking into it."

"I'm glad to hear this. Like I said, I'm certain that you're the one who finds him and stops him."

"I may already have. It's in the agent's hands now. If I was able to be a part of this, then I did my part." Jack suddenly remembered the research he had done earlier that day. "Speaking of which, I have something for you to look at."

He stood up and crossed the room to his desk where he retrieved his notebook. As he walked back over to Shelby, he pulled out the photo of the house that he had found at the Cleveland Public Library and handed it to her.

"Does this place look familiar at all to you?"

It was like a wave of shock washed over Shelby's face as she viewed the picture.

"That's it!" she said with astonishment. "That's where he took me. I'm certain of it. I never saw the front of the house, but I remember those big windows. They were on all sides."

"You were kept in the basement. At what point did you see the windows?"

"On the last night that I was there. I remember it now. I was half-asleep I think. He walked me outside and I saw those tall, leaded glass windows. The whole house was stone. And that barn too, I remember it as well. It was night, but I remember that I was able to see that weather vane on top."

"I was trying to figure out what that was," Jack said as he took a closer look at the photo.

"It's a chicken. I thought how odd it was that someone would have a weather vane of a chicken on their barn."

"Did you go into the barn?"

"No. I walked right past it."

"Where did he take you, Shelby?"

"I don't know."

"If he didn't take you into the barn, he must have taken you somewhere. Was it into the woods?"

"No. It wasn't into the woods."

"A field?"

"It had dirt. There was a lot of really dry dirt."

"Like in a barn?"

"He didn't take me into the barn!"

Jack noticed that she was shaking. It was time to quit.

"Okay. Let's not think about it. Let's put it out of mind for now."

"Jack, I should go."

"But you've only just gotten here."

"I know, but I need to clear my head and think."

"Will I see you tomorrow?"

Shelby could tell that Jack was getting upset.

"Yes," she calmly told him after a moment, "you'll see me tomorrow night. I promise you."

And with that, Shelby gave him another small kiss and descended the stairs. Jack worried that he had pushed her a little too hard to remember an event in her life that she had obviously spent the last fifteen years trying to forget. He didn't want to scare her away and decided at once that he'd never put her on the spot again. He'd have to be more tactful in the future.

Chapter 16

Jack had fallen asleep the previous evening with his windows left wide open and awoke to a warm breeze blowing across his bedroom. It was going to be a day just like the last: mild, beautiful and sunny. Again he thought about taking advantage of the fine weather. There wasn't that much for him to do at this point. The case was now in the hands of the FBI and with some luck, he'd be hearing from Special Agent Andrew Spurlock by the end of the day. Hopefully he'd have a suspect in custody. Still, he thought, it wouldn't hurt to do a little more research of his own.

After shaving and taking a shower, Jack dressed and drove up to the gas station to get himself a cup of coffee and a couple of donuts. He returned home and watched the morning news. There was no mention of the Rebecca Lowe case. It was more to do with the coming elections and the World Series, which the Cleveland Indians had recently been knocked out of contention for. According to the weatherman, the warm temperatures would be sticking around for another day. A cold front was expected to cross the region the following evening, bringing a chance of storms. Jack smiled at this. He always loved a good thunderstorm.

Once the news was over, Jack strolled over to his desk, booted up his laptop and connected to the internet. He cleared his head and put on a CD by Mossy Moran, one of his favorite local Irish musicians. Jack figured that he'd begin by checking into his two suspects: Mr. Dresden's driver and Percy Stuart. He'd start with Mr. Stuart.

He linked to the Cuyahoga County Recorder's website. Here, he found a number of real estate transactions that concerned Mr. Stuart. The list started in the late 1970's with the most recent for a property in Solon, purchased just two months ago. There seemed to be something of a lull in activity between 1997 and 2006, with only a couple of properties passing through his ownership during this time. Jack thought that he would take another approach.

He typed Percy Stuart's name into a search on social networking website. There were quite a few names that came up. Jack began to sort through them one at a time. Eventually, he lucked out and located the right one. He looked towards the bottom of the page and found Mr. Stuart's past companies listed. From 1982 to 1986, he was the operation's manager for Bright-Way Materials Handling. Then, in 1988, he founded Stuart Shipping and Handling. He continued to operate this company until 1997, at which time he sold the firm to a larger group out of Pittsburgh.

Pittsburgh; now that was something. Jack glanced over at the stack of articles that Shelby had given him. Pittsburgh was the next location that the kidnapper had struck. This began in 1995: two full years before the company was sold. Still, it was possible that Percy Stuart already had dealings that took him there prior to his company's sale. The next affiliation was with a company called Torrent. There weren't many details listed as to what this business was or where it was located, though it likely had something to do with shipping. He was listed as vice-president of operations from 2001 to 2003. The last company listed was Burton Freight of Solon. It named him as co-owner from 2006 to the present. This was his current company. There were many gaps in his residency here in Cleveland, but it wasn't enough to convict: only to suspect even further.

His next search took him to Claude Dresden's driver. Jack didn't even know the man's name, so he thought that he would attempt a reverse directory search. He typed in Mr. Dresden's address and came up with two results. Claude Dresden, obviously, and a man named Douglas Palmer. This had to be Mr. Dresden's chauffeur. He remembered the driver mentioning that he had just moved back to the area about a half a year earlier. He had claimed to have been a merchant marine and that he worked mostly out of Louisiana. Jack did a quick search on a social networking site, but came up with nothing. He thought he'd give MySpace a try, but again there was no page listed. He next typed Douglas Palmer's name into a genealogical site and found quite a few listings for people with that name. One of these matched a man of about his age living in Slidell, Louisiana for the last six years. Unfortunately, this meant that he didn't fit the suspect's profile of recently living in Kansas or San Francisco. It was possible that he had traveled to these locations. Jack remembered what it was like when he was a merchant marine on the Great Lakes. It meant a lot of traveling. He certainly would have been able to afford to do this, as it was a higher paying job.

So far, it all seemed to be a series of dead ends. There wasn't enough to go on. Both Mr. Palmer and Mr. Stuart could have been absent from Northeast Ohio during the time that the other girls were kidnapped from the other states, but there was no definite way of knowing exactly where they were. He could only hope that Special Agent Spurlock would have more luck.

That afternoon, Jack did some running around. It was mostly mundane tasks such as grocery shopping and going to the bank. He did make a stop at around three up at McNamara's for a pint of Guinness. The front door was propped wide open, as was the one leading out to the back patio. A warm breeze blew through the empty bar. With the exception of Positive Bill the bartender, the place was deserted. The after-work crowd wouldn't start showing up until around four. Jack wasn't planning on staying quite that long though. He and Bill chatted for a while about their normal topics of conversation: music, sports and work. Also, it turned out that Bill had met a young lady a couple of nights earlier and things looked promising. Jack decided against mentioning Shelby. Too many times in the past, he'd found himself in a relationship and would tell his friends about it. Unfortunately, these turned out to just be flings that only lasted a few days. He wasn't very superstitious, but thought on occasion that by talking about it so much he had jinxed the whole thing. He definitely didn't want that to be the case with Shelby.

Bill had briefly asked Jack about the new scrapes on his face, but Jack danced around giving him a straight answer. He didn't want anyone to know about the case he'd been working. He'd tell them eventually, but wanted to wait until it was over.

As he finished his pint, his friends Rick and Michelle walked in. He was in something of a hurry to get home and felt bad that he wouldn't have the chance to catch up with them. Rick worked odd hours and they didn't get to see that much of each other. A good conversation with them would have to wait. As Jack paid his tab, Rick noticed his face.

"What happened to you?" he asked.

"Nothing. Tripped going up the steps."

"Going *up* the steps, now that's a first. Oh, are you still having your Halloween party this Friday?"

The thought had completely slipped Jack's mind. It was already Tuesday and Halloween was the next day. He wouldn't hold a party such as that during the middle of the week and always held it on the closest weekend evening. That would have been that coming Friday night.

"Yeah," Jack replied. "It should be Friday at around seven."

"Are ya getting a keg or is it BYOB?"

Jack would've loved to have picked up a keg of beer, but the last time he had done this, it was for his St. Patrick's Day party and he'd purchased a keg of Great Lakes Conway's Irish Ale. The only problem with this was that the alcohol content in this beverage was quite high. The party started at eight and was over by a little passed ten. Everyone got so inebriated that within a couple of hours they were either fighting with each other or throwing up in the front yard.

"I think we'll go the route of BYOB this time," Jack informed him. "Last time I bought the beer, it was a disaster."

"Oh yeah. I remember that," Rick said as though reaching for a distant memory.

Jack waived goodbye and started for the door.

"I'll see you all on Friday night then."

With that, Jack walked out, got into his car and drove home.

Jack wasn't home ten minutes before his doorbell rang. It was a quarter after four: too early for it to have been Shelby. He walked to the bottom of the first set of stairs and opened the door. Through the front door below, he could see Special Agent Andrew Spurlock standing on his front porch. He descended the next set of steps and let him in.

"Good afternoon Agent Spurlock," Jack greeted. "How are you doing today?"

"I'm well. May I come in?"

"Certainly."

Jack and the agent walked upstairs and into Jack's living room. The agent took a seat on the couch and pulled out his notepad.

"Well," he began, "I guess I'll get right to it. I checked out both of your suspects today, Percy Stuart and Doug Palmer: that's Mr. Dresden's driver's name."

"I know," Jack interrupted. "I looked him up earlier today."

"I see. Well, I have to tell you that both of them have alibis for their whereabouts on Saturday evening."

"Really?"

"Really. Percy Stuart was with his wife and children all night. His wife vouched for that. He came home at six thirty on Saturday evening and didn't leave the house again until nine the following morning, and that was to go to church."

"Hmm," Jack pensively considered. "What about Douglas Palmer?"

"He was in Toledo that night."

"And his alibi?"

"Mr. Dresden. They left Chagrin Falls at around four in the afternoon and arrived in Toledo sometime around six thirty. They were visiting Claude Dresden's sister: something about wanting to show her some trunk of magic tricks or something. The last time Mr. Dresden saw Mr. Palmer that evening was just before he turned in: sometime around ten. You said that you were attacked just before eleven. That would have given him about an hour to drive back to Lakewood. He'd have had to have been driving close to 150 miles an hour in order to have pulled that off."

"And I was so certain that it would have been one of those two."

"They're the only ones that you mentioned this case to?"

"The only ones that seemed to fit the bill."

"I want you to think really hard. Who else did you talk to?"

Jack thought back to the night that he and Shelby were trying to come up with possible suspects.

"Aside from my cousins Pam and Trish, there was Lauren Call. I'm certain that she would have mentioned our conversation to her husband, but I can't see why he would attack me. I also spoke with her mother-in-law, but that wouldn't make sense either."

"No. It wouldn't," Agent Spurlock agreed. "Is there anyone else?"

"Oh, I also spoke with the assistant principal at Lauren Call's former high school."

"What was his name?"

"Haas, I believe."

Agent Spurlock jotted this down in his notepad.

"Come to think of it," Jack continued, "He did mention that he was working at the school when she was attacked. I think he said he was a phys-ed teacher at the time. You know? I did have a theory going for a time that this kidnapper knew his victims, but I couldn't back it up with anything."

"Still, it merits looking into. I'll run a check on him after I get back to the office."

"The only other person that springs to mind is Sheriff's Deputy Lauber."

Agent Spurlock closed his notepad.

"And that would make absolutely no sense either," he declared. "It was Deputy Lauber that called my office and informed us of your activities. Why would he alert us to this case if he was the one who was behind these kidnappings?"

"I know. I already scratched him off my list of suspects. I still can't help but wonder who else at the sheriff's department knows about this."

"We prefer not to suspect law enforcement officials, but if it makes you feel any better, I'll contact Deputy Lauber and ask him if he shared this information with anyone else."

"I appreciate that."

"I'll start by looking into this assistant principal that you mentioned. In the meantime, I don't want you to have any further contact with Mr. Palmer or Mr. Stuart. I'd also appreciate it if you kept clear of this Haas guy."

"I have no reason to call any of them. Mr. Dresden and I have concluded our business together. I've already made my follow-up visit to him."

"Good," the agent retorted. "Do you still have my card?"

"I do."

"Well, don't hesitate to use it."

"I won't. Thanks. I'll see you to the door."

"That's okay. I can see myself out."

With that, Agent Spurlock descended the stairs and exited the apartment. A moment later, Jack heard the front door close tightly. Things, he thought, weren't looking that good.

Sometime just after seven, Jack's cell phone rang. He looked at the caller I.D. and saw that the number was from a Cleveland exchange. He answered it with curiosity.

"Hello?"

"Hi Jack, it's Pam. How are you doing?"

"Pam. Not too bad. How have you been?"

"Keeping pretty busy, which brings me to why I called."

"The case?"

"I've been on the phone quite a bit over this since early Monday morning, sending emails, faxes of photos, physical descriptions and case reviews."

"Were you able to make a match?"

"Jack, it doesn't look promising. I started on Sunday evening by comparing the articles you gave me with what we have on our database. Hardly anything really seemed to match up with the time frame for when these girls went missing. We had a few but their ethnicity didn't match up. I sent them out nonetheless. I also stumbled across a couple of "unidentifieds" from the late eighties but that predates the cases that you're looking into."

"What were their causes of death?"

"Hold on a second and I'll get their files." There was a long pause. Jack flipped on his television and turned to the weather. He briefly caught the extended forecast and saw that it was calling for thunderstorms the following evening. A moment later, Pam had returned to the phone. "According to the case files, it was originally thought that they died from blunt force trauma to the head, but following the autopsies, it was determined that they both died from asphyxiation due to strangulation."

"Blunt force trauma; it wouldn't happen to be to the *back* of the head, would it?"

Pam glanced at the page for a moment.

"As a matter of fact, it is. How did you know that?"

"Hit possibly by a flashlight?"

"Yeah, that's one possibility, I guess. What are you getting at?"

Jack couldn't believe it.

"This bastard *did* strike before," he informed her. "It was the same with the others. He rendered them unconscious by striking them with a flashlight then kidnapped them. You said they were strangled?"

"That's right."

"Now that's something new. Trish had figured that his past victims were likely murdered. We just didn't know how he killed them. When were they discovered?"

"March of 1989."

"At the same time?"

"Both girls were discovered at the edge of a pasture."

"What, just lying on the ground?"

"No, their remains were unearthed when a rancher went to bury one of his horses that had died. According to the files, he had dug down with his backhoe about three feet before reaching the first set of remains. They were wrapped up in a couple of black garbage bags. He reported the discovery right away and the police came in and tore up the whole area. The second victim was discovered later that evening. This is weird; it says that the pit was lined with branches and sticks. The excavation continued for another three days and after the cadaver dogs couldn't locate anything else, the search was called off."

"Where was this pasture located?"

"Let me see." Pam scanned the file for a moment. There was a long pause.

"Pam?"

"I'm, still here," she replied, but grew silent once again.

"What is it?"

"I should have seen this before."

"Let me take a wild guess. Greeley Township?"

"Yes, Jack. Greeley Township."

"Is there an address?"

Pam looked further down the page.

"3989 Indianola Road."

"That's just up the road from the Rainey House. Trish was so close. She was off by just a bit."

"Jack, Trish is never off by 'just a bit.' You know as well

as I do that she's always dead on. If she says that they were taken to that Rainey place, then that's where they were taken. That doesn't necessarily mean that their bodies were dumped there."

"But the house was unoccupied throughout the early nineties."

"All the better a place to take someone. Think about it."

Jack did. It all made sense.

"You said that they searched the area and didn't come up with anything more than two bodies?"

"That's right," Pam told him.

"And they didn't fit the descriptions of anyone missing from the area?"

"No. It was estimated that they had been dead for close to four years. We didn't have any missing persons cases that fit from that time frame."

"Did you check with other metropolitan areas across the region?"

"Jack, we didn't have the technologies that we have today. There was no DNA testing back then and the internet was still something that was being developed. If they had been found today, they would have been entered into a huge database and we'd have certainly had a match right away. As it is, there aren't any genetic samples that were taken. We held onto the remains for quite some time, hoping that someone would come forward to claim them, but after no one did, they were cremated and their ashes were interred in a city cemetery."

"Well, they had to come from somewhere."

"I'll tell you what," Pam began. "I'll take the files and enter them into the database and send them out tomorrow morning to every major city within five hundred miles."

"That sounds like it'll take some time."

"Not really. It's just a matter of entering all of the information into the computer. It's all stuff that should have been done years ago anyway."

"Pam, I can't tell you how much this all means to me."

"Come on. We're family. We help each other out like this. I'll let you know if I come up with anything."

"Thanks Pam. I'll talk to you soon. Give my love to your mom."

"I will."

"And you take care."

"Thanks. You too."

Jack ended his call faced with new questions. Until a few hours ago, he was certain that Percy Stuart was somehow connected, but Agent Spurlock had told him that Mr. Stuart had an alibi for his whereabouts on Saturday night. This new information concerning Greeley Township though pointed the finger at him once more. Perhaps, Jack thought, he was looking at this from the wrong angle. Just because Mr. Stuart owned the property didn't necessarily mean that he was involved. Perhaps the killer, and it was now safe to call him one, simply knew that the Rainey House was vacant. It could have been anyone. Things weren't adding up and Jack was starting to get a headache. He needed to step away from it for a while. Maybe he'd get some new ideas if he did.

Jack awoke at around eleven o'clock to the sound of his doorbell ringing. He had dozed off at some point on the couch with the television still tuned in to the weather. He sat up, wiped the sleep from his eyes and turned the television off. He descended the steps and opened the door at the bottom. Standing on the porch below was Shelby. He raced down, threw the bolt and let her in.

"You look like you just woke up," she said as she crossed the threshold.

"I did. How can you tell?"

"Your hair's standing up a bit."

"Oh." Jack quickly ran his right hand through his hair, flattening it out. "That better?"

"Much."

They walked up to Jack's apartment. As soon as they reached the top of the stairs, Shelby turned around suddenly, grabbed Jack by the shirt, threw him against the wall and began to passionately kiss him. He immediately felt as though he were about to fall into a swoon. The whole room went blurry and the next thing he knew, he was lying under a blanket on the couch with Shelby pressed tightly against him. He looked at the clock on the wall above his television set and saw that it was well after two in the morning. He had no memory of what had just happened or where the time had gone. Shelby stirred and looked up at him with her bright blue eyes.

"You're awake," she said as she caressed her hand across his chest.

"Yeah, I'm..." Jack couldn't even complete his words before Shelby was kissing him again. After a few moments, she slowly pulled her lips away and smiled.

"You were about to say?"

"I can't remember." Jack's mind had gone completely blank. He couldn't figure out what it was about Shelby that had such an affect on him. Maybe it was love, he thought.

"Oh. Well, how did it go today?"

Jack suddenly remembered the conversation he'd had with the federal agent and the call from Pam.

"Not too good. I met with Special Agent Spurlock earlier."

"What did he have to say?"

"Well, it turns out that both Percy Stuart and Mr. Dresden's driver have alibis for where they were on Saturday night."

"That's not good." Shelby had another thought. "Is it possible that they had hired someone to attack you?"

"Not likely. I have the feeling that this person works alone and wouldn't want to draw attention to themselves by involving a second party."

"I can see that."

"The only other person that comes to mind as a suspect is assistant principal Haas. Agent Spurlock is going to run a check on him."

"I thought we already ruled him out."

"Not quite. Besides, he's the only other person that knew I was on this case. I mean, who else could it be?"

"Did you try to find anything out on him?"

"No. I'm leaving it up to the feds. Oh, there was something else. I heard back from Pam this evening. She didn't have any matches between their Jane Does and anyone missing from the other areas that this guy had struck."

"This really isn't good. It looks like we're back to square one."

"Well, not entirely. The county morgue did have a couple of unidentified females come in back in the late 80's. They had

142

trauma wounds to the back of their heads and both were killed by being strangled."

"That seems to fit. The head wounds, I mean."

"There's more. Their bodies were discovered near the edge of a pasture in Greeley Township."

"Where in Greeley Township?"

"Indianola Road. It's right up the street from the Rainey House."

"Are you telling me that this guy had killed before?"

"Long before by the looks of it. They figured that these girls had been dead for about four years, which would place their disappearance some time around 1985."

"That long ago?"

"Here's the real kicker. They don't match up with anyone missing from the area during that time. Pam's going to enter their information into some database and see if she can find a match that way."

"We're running out of time, Jack."

"What do you mean?"

"Tomorrow's the 31st. That will be two weeks since Rebecca Lowe went missing."

Jack had completely forgotten about their time limit.

"I don't know what else I can do. I've pretty much exhausted all of my resources. Still, I feel like there's something that I'm missing here; like it's right under my nose and I just can't see it."

Jack sat up and rubbed his eyes. He was about to get up and go to his desk to get his notebook, but Shelby placed a hand on his shoulder.

"Please," she said. "Lie back down with me."

Jack gave her a curious look.

"Are you okay?" he asked.

"Yeah, I just want you to hold me for a while."

Jack obliged and rested himself back down beside her. She wrapped her arms about him and snuggled in closely. Jack began to slowly drift off to sleep. Just as he was losing consciousness, he heard her whisper quietly into his ear.

"Jack, I think I'm falling in love with you."

Chapter 17

Jack awoke under a blanket on his couch. It was well past noon and Shelby Tomlinson was gone. As he lay there, he thought about what she had said to him the previous evening. She'd mentioned something about being back at square one. Maybe that's what he needed to do. Maybe he needed to start at the beginning and go through everything that he had. The day was wasting away. He needed to start immediately.

He got up, folded the blanket and put it back in the closet. Remembering that it was supposed to be a beautiful day, quite possibly the last one until spring, he walked about the apartment and opened all of the windows. A warm and gusty breeze blew his curtains about. He flipped on the television for a few minutes and caught the weather. The entire area was under a high wind warning until midnight.

Jack suddenly remembered that it was Halloween: one of his favorite holidays. Back when he'd lived in Avon Lake, he used to set up his front yard to look like an old run-down cemetery. It really was quite a display. He'd built a rickety white picket fence to go around the property and placed small wooden crosses and sandstone blocks about, arranged to look like ancient tombstones. He'd acquired these stone blocks some years earlier when a bell tower was torn down on his old church in Cleveland. He'd set up this cemetery around the beginning of October and would leave it up until after his Halloween party. When not being used as tombstones, the sandstone blocks were utilized for landscaping around the yard.

His house was always the one that the kids were afraid to approach on Halloween night. It became an annual challenge for them to go and get candy from the house with the graveyard. Perhaps it was the scary music that Jack played or the creepy lights and fog machine he employed that kept them at bay. Most likely though, it was the fact that Jack would put on drywall stilts that made him nine feet tall, drape himself with cloaks and black sheets, place a real pumpkin on his head and walk around the yard.

The last time he'd done this was two years ago. He'd been renting the house from his parents: the house he'd grown up in. In

2005, his father retired and moved with his mother out to the summer place on Catawba Island. It was a seasonal cottage, but recently had been converted into a year-round residence. They sold the house in Avon Lake and Jack moved to Lakewood. Sometimes he missed the old place, but he liked his apartment all the same.

As Jack turned off the television, he thought about running up to the store to buy a pumpkin but didn't see much sense in it. He hadn't handed out candy once since moving to Lakewood, but did enjoy roasting pumpkin seeds. He'd likely spend the evening with his brother, taking his nieces and nephews out for trick-or-treating, while his sister-in-law handed out candy at their place. He'd give a call after while to see what their plans were.

Jack walked over to his desk and booted up his laptop. He pulled out the file folder and notebook that he'd been keeping his notes in. Next, he retrieved the photograph of the Rainey House and set that on the desk. Lastly, he placed the reconstructed flashlight lens with the other articles that he had pulled out. The answer was right here in front of him. Somehow, these all fit together.

He turned to his laptop, got online and began to do general searches at random on small bits of info related to this case. He hoped that maybe while doing this he'd stumble onto something or at least come up with a better idea as to how to approach the situation. He typed in *Frank Rainey House*, but there really wasn't that much he could find; just a listing that named it as a demolished residence in Greeley Township. He next typed *Fleur-de-lis Estates*, but only came up with listings for houses for sale. This was getting him nowhere. He even tried *Witch Hazel*. Aside from bringing up a page for a band with that name, it just gave him a description of the plant and it's uses.

He next tried searches on the missing girls from around Cleveland. He typed in the names *Melanie Maguire, Kellie Ripley, Nadine Somerset,* and *Anne Perkins*. He'd come across that last name somewhere recently. He thought about it for a moment and remembered that the Perkins family originally owned the Rainey property, but that was nearly a century and a half ago. This was just one of those odd coincidences. His search on these four girls only brought up their missing person's profiles with the Center for

145

Missing and Exploited Children. There was nothing new here.

He then was struck with an idea. He'd been so concerned with who it was that owned the Rainey House at the time of the disappearances, that being Percy Stuart. Maybe he needed to go back just a bit further. He referred back to his notes and located the names of the previous owners. Quickly, he typed *Archibald A. Swift* into the Cleveland News Index and came up with an obituary date of June 24, 1989. He wrote this down in his notebook. It would mean another trip to the Fairview Park Public Library.

He next typed *Robert Vaule* into the necrology file and found his obituary abstract from 1949. It listed his wife as Gertrude, but not much else. Still, he wrote down the date for this as well. Maybe there would be more in his actual obituary from the newspaper.

He logged off, shut down his laptop and gathered his notes together. He picked up his keys and grabbed his patchwork Irish wool cap from the newel post at the top of his stairs and was out the door in a flash.

As he made his way out to Fairview Park, he placed a brief call to his brother.

"Mike," he said as a deep male voice had answered on the other end of the line.

"Jack? Haven't heard from you in a while. I was beginning to wonder if you'd fallen off the face of the Earth again."

Jack was known to lay low for long periods of time: especially when working on a big project.

"I'm still here. Just been really busy. How have you been?"

"Not bad. Keeping busy with work. Speaking of which, I heard that you were in New York recently."

"Yeah. I had to go there to purchase a trunk for a client."

"How did that go?"

"It was alright. I got to do a little bit of sightseeing."

"Are you still sick?"

"Na. I've been feeling better these last few days."

"Good. Do you want to come over this evening and take the kids out with me?"

"Yeah, I don't see why not."

"Cool. It's from six to seven thirty. Come over a bit earlier if you want. It'll give us a chance to catch up a bit."

"You got it. I'll shoot over sometime around five."

"Five it is. See you then."

Jack hung up the phone and put it in the cup holder in the center console. Sometimes it was hard for him to retrieve it from his pocket while he was driving. He'd missed too many calls that way. Placing it here made it much easier to answer, should anyone call. He continued on to the library with his driver's side window down all the way. The warm air that rushed past him was exhilarating. He knew this fine weather wouldn't last.

Jack arrived at the Fairview Park Public Library sometime just before two. He immediately set himself to the task of locating the microfilm reels relevant to the obituaries he needed. He started with Robert Vaule's in the Cleveland Press from November 2, 1949. After loading the microfilm viewer, he began to scan through the images until he found the right date and page. He browsed the column and soon located it.

> *Vaule, Robert R. Beloved husband of Gertrude (nee Forrest). November 1ˢᵗ, 1949 at residence. Friends received at Usher and Swift Funeral Chapel Tuesday from 1 to 3pm. 324 South Camden St. Greeley Township. Funeral services from St. Gregory's Church Wednesday at 11am. Burial to follow at Holy Trinity Cemetery in Westerland.*

Jack zoomed in on the obituary and printed it out. There wasn't much here for him to go on. Something struck him as curious about this write-up though. It was the name of the funeral home: Usher and Swift. He couldn't help but wonder how common the name *Swift* was.

He rewound the film, unloaded it, put it back into its respective box and placed it in the return tray. He then walked over to another filing cabinet and retrieved a roll of film from The Plain Dealer that was marked as being from June of 1989. He loaded it into the viewer and sped through the film until he nearly reached the end of the reel. He stopped and looked at the date on the page. It read June 22nd. He slowly advanced the film until he came to the date of the 24th. He continued into section B and found the obituaries on page 3. Carefully, Jack scanned the columns until he found Mr. Swift's death notice.

> *Swift, Archibald A., 77, Husband of the late Maureen (nee Hubbard). Entered into rest on June 23rd following a lengthy illness. Member of the Knights of Saint Peter, American Legion and SAR. Long time proprietor of the A. A. Swift Funeral Chapel. Survivors include his daughters Helen Swift of Lorain and Claire Swift of Bainbridge. Services to be held at the A. A. Swift Funeral Chapel, 324 S. Camden Street, Greeley Township, Thursday at 11am. Burial to follow at Greeley Twp. Cemetery.*

Jack printed out the obituary and gave it another look. There was no coincidence here. It had to be the same Swift that had owned the funeral home with Usher that Mr. Vaule was buried out of. The address was the same. Jack unloaded the viewer and placed the reel in the return tray. He gathered his notebook and the printouts that he'd just made and left the library. He got into his car and headed for home. It was nearly three thirty. He'd have to hurry if he was going to make it over to his brother's by five.

For the past few years, Jack had been dressing as The Ghoul: a former late night horror movie host who had become something of a local pop icon. He'd have to dig out his lab coat and fright wig from the back of the closet. It would also take about twenty minutes for him to apply the fake goatee.

Jack got on Interstate 90 at the Hilliard Road entrance but was smart enough to do the speed limit. Just over the rise was one of the better-known speed traps in the area, second only to the one in Linndale on Interstate 71. Jack didn't need to worry though as there was no police car in sight. He thought for a few moments about the articles he had just printed out. For some reason, he kept coming back to the obituary for Archibald Swift. Mr. Swift had been a funeral director. Jack wondered how anyone could have possibly wanted to go into that line of work. It seemed really creepy. Just then, he remembered that someone had told him recently that it wasn't as creepy as he would think. Who was it that had told him that? He suddenly had a flash of grabbing at a strap on a body bag and being told to take a firm grasp of the feet. It was a middle-aged man. A mortician. The man he'd met at the morgue. Bob... something. At that moment, another image came to him. It was of Bob looking down at the files that Pam had set on her desk. Someone else did know that he was working on that case. He just didn't tell the person about it. They'd figured it out on their own.

Jack slammed on the brakes and pulled over. He couldn't believe it. He pulled out his notebook and retrieved the sketch of the killer that he'd made based off of Trish's description. It was the same man, about fifteen years older, but the same man nonetheless. Jack stopped for a moment and thought about it. He didn't know anything about this man. Pam seemed to know him well enough. They seemed quite friendly with each other. Perhaps he was wrong. Maybe he wanted Bob to be the same man in the drawing and was only seeing what he wanted to see. He took another look at the sketch. The resemblance was uncanny. He placed the drawing back into his notebook, pulled out into traffic and continued home as fast as he could.

Jack arrived at his place around four that afternoon. He parked the car in the driveway and raced up the stairs to his apartment. He set the notebook on his desk, pulled out his phone and made a call. The phone rang three times before there was an answer.

"Hello?"

"Pam, it's Jack."

"Hi Jack," she replied. "I was about to call you. I entered those two Jane Doe cases into the database and think I may have found a match. They may be from Buffalo, New York."

"That's great, but not the reason that I'm calling."

"Oh? What is it? You sound flustered."

"And for a good reason. I need you to tell me everything that you know about Bob."

"Bob?"

"Yeah, you know. Bob the mortician that came up to the morgue when I was there."

"Oh, Bob Woodring."

Woodring. That was the name that Jack was trying to remember.

"Yes. That's him. What do you know about him?"

"Oh, he's a nice guy. Quiet. Kind of keeps to himself a bit. Not too bad on the eyes either, I guess."

"Okay, how long have you known him?"

"Oh gosh, a long time I guess."

"Damn." Jack realized that if she knew him for a long time that he likely lived in the area for years.

"I first met him when he was just starting off in the industry. Worked for a couple of different families."

"Hmm." Jack was perplexed.

"I thought he was going to end up taking over one of the companies, but he abruptly moved away."

"What?"

"Yeah, he just moved back a few months ago."

"Do you remember if he ever happened to work at a funeral home named A. A. Swift?"

"Swift? Yeah but that was a long time ago. How did you know that?"

"And do you remember where that funeral home was located?"

There was a long pause. After a few moments, Pam spoke up.

"Jack, I think I know where you're going with this and I think you're wrong. Bob's a good man."

"It all makes sense to me now. Bob Woodring worked for Swift until when?"

"He was there until the old man passed away: sometime in the late 80's I think."

"It was 1989. When did he move away?"

"Early 90's."

"Could it have possibly been 1993?"

"It could have been."

"Look. The Rainey House was owned by Mr. Swift. After Mr. Swift died, Bob knew that it was unoccupied. It was the perfect place to have taken those girls. One got away in May of 1993, one that could describe him. He decided to move at once before he was found out. He drove around an older luxury car. I'm guessing that it was a former funeral vehicle, used for smaller families when a limo wasn't needed. The chemical smell that was reported to accompany this man, I'm wondering if it might be something like embalming fluid. It was described as reminding someone of biology class."

"This all sounds a little coincidental."

"Not when you take into account the fact that I was attacked on Saturday night by someone who knew I was working this case and wanted me off of it, or better yet, dead."

"Did you tell him what you were working on? I sure didn't."

"Neither of us did, nor did we need to. You set the files down on your desk when you went to go and get a body from the cooler. He saw the files, Pam."

"Oh God…"

"What?"

"I can't believe it."

"Believe what?"

Pam paused for a moment before answering.

"He asked me about you after you had left."

"What did he ask?"

There was another long pause.

"I'm sorry Jack. He asked me what part of town you were from and I told him."

"Well, I guess that's how he found me."

"I am really, really sorry. You know that I wouldn't…"

"It's okay, Pam. You didn't know. Neither did I."

"I just can't believe it'd be him."

"Like you said, he just moved back a few months ago. Do you know where he lives?"

"Not exactly. I mean I've never been out to his place or anything like that. When he first came back to the area and started at Kollifer's, he told me that he'd moved into his Uncle Max's old house out in Parkington."

"Parkington? That's a pretty rural area. Kind of a haul to get out there too."

151

"It's not that far from the funeral home he works for."

"Just another thought," Jack added. "Do you remember where he lived before first coming to Cleveland."

"Wait a minute. I didn't tell you that he wasn't originally from Cleveland."

"I know, but he's not. Is he?"

"No Jack, he's not."

"He's from Buffalo, Right?"

"Yes."

"Thought so. Look, I've got to go here. There's something I have to look up and a few phone calls that I need to make. Can you do me a favor and not mention this to anyone?"

"I won't say a word. But what if he stops by? That's going to be a bit uncomfortable to say the least."

"Are you expecting him?"

"No."

"Then I wouldn't worry. With luck, this will all be over before the end of the night. Take care, Pam and be safe."

"Thanks, Jack. You too."

Jack hung up and quickly made another brief call to his brother explaining that he wouldn't be able to make it over for trick-or-treating. When asked why, Jack simply told him that it had to do with work and that he'd tell him all about it another time.

After concluding his call with his brother, Jack booted up his laptop and jumped online. He went directly to the white pages and typed in the name *Robert Woodring* with a location for *Parkington*. No listing came up. He thought that he'd just try *Woodring* for the same location, just in case Robert wasn't his real first name, but again there was no match. Pam had said that he was living at his Uncle Max's old house, but this didn't necessarily mean that Woodring was his Uncle Max's last name. Jack quickly found the county marriage index. He typed in the name *Woodring* for the bride's name and hit enter. There were only a few matches that came up but only one of them, a woman named Lucille Woodring, had married a man named Maxwell Stone. Jack went back to the white pages and typed in *Maxwell Stone* and *Parkington*. Nothing came up. He tried his regular genealogical website and entered Maxwell Stone's name in the search. He finally got a hit. Only one name and address came up. It was for

Maxwell Stone at 7076 Weymouth Road in Parkington, Ohio. Jack wrote this down in his notebook. He scoured his desk until he located Special Agent Andrew Spurlock's card. He quickly dialed the cell phone number that was written on the back.

"Spurlock," the voice declared on the other end.

"Agent Spurlock, It's Jack Sullivan."

"Ah, Mr. Sullivan. I spoke with assistant principal Haas earlier…"

"That's nice, but it's not him."

"Actually," the agent continued, "He doesn't have an alibi for his whereabouts on Saturday night and does seem to fit the profile of the man we've been looking for. We're considering bringing him in for further questioning. Looks like you were right."

"Forget it. It's not him."

"If not him, then who?"

"Bob Woodring."

"And who is Bob Woodring?"

"He's a mortician out in Parkington. He knew I was working this case and had found out just a few hours before I was attacked. He used to work for Swift Funeral Home out in Greeley Township. Mr. Swift once owned the old Rainey House. After Swift died, Woodring knew it was empty and was taking these girls out there. That's where he killed them. There was also the discovery of two bodies on a piece of land just up the road from there back in the late 80's. He moved away from the area right after Lauren Call's near abduction and just moved back a few months ago. It all fits."

"I don't know Jack. This Haas guy really seems to be a pretty good suspect."

"And I'm telling you that it's Woodring. I'm certain of it."

"Okay. So where is this Bob Woodring now?"

"He lives at 7076 Weymouth Road."

"And that's in Parkington, you said?"

"That's right."

"Fine. I'll drive out there in the morning and question him as well."

"We can't wait until the morning. It's already been fourteen days since Rebecca Lowe has gone missing. She won't be alive by the morning."

"Fourteen days? What's that got to do with anything?"

"It's a long story, but trust me. You have to go there now."

"Mr. Sullivan, you sound overly excited. You need to calm down and take it easy."

"I'm not going to take it easy and if you're not going to go out there and take care of this, then I will."

"Mr. Sullivan…"

Jack hung up the phone and put it in his pocket. He did a quick search online for 7076 Weymouth Road in Parkington, Ohio. He located it in no time, made a printout of the directions, logged off and shut down his laptop.

Before he left, he looked about his apartment and tried to find something that he could use as a weapon, should there be a confrontation. He suddenly remembered the tire iron that he'd carried upstairs with him a couple of days earlier. He hadn't taken it back out to his car yet and it was now in his coat closet; a grand place to have it if he should happen to get a flat tire. He opened the closet, picked up the tire iron and was out the door. As he walked to his car, his cell phone began to ring. It was Agent Spurlock calling him back: likely trying to deter him from driving out there. Jack didn't answer. He opened the driver's side door of his Mazda and tossed the tire iron on the front passenger's seat. A strong gust of wind suddenly kicked up, bringing down a shower of gold and red leaves. The skies to the west were growing heavy with storm clouds and a faint roll of thunder could be heard rumbling off in the distance. Amid all of this, Jack felt bad for his brother's kids.

Their Halloween might get rained out

Chapter 18

Parkington was located along the eastern border of Cuyahoga County and the drive from Jack's apartment took just over an hour to make. He arrived at 7076 Weymouth Road at about a quarter to six. The area was quite rural, as Jack figured it would be. He stopped his car at the end of the driveway for a moment to get a look at the house. There was nothing particularly interesting about it. It was a small green and white bungalow that sat on a fairly sizable tract of land, not very wide, but quite deep by the looks of it. There weren't any houses in the immediate area and it seemed like a perfect place to take someone without anyone knowing.

It was getting quite dark out. Not only was the sun going down, but the coming storm had also followed Jack the entire way. There would be no sunset. In spite of the growing darkness, Jack noticed that there were no lights on in the house. Perhaps Bob Woodring wasn't home, he thought. Still, he didn't want to risk it. He needed the element of surprise and Bob already knew what his car looked like. Parking in the driveway was out of the question. He put the Mazda back into gear and continued down the road. He stopped again about a quarter of a mile from the house and parked at the side of the road along a dense patch of woods. He grabbed the tire iron and stepped out of the vehicle but decided not to lock it, as he didn't want the horn to beep. That might draw unwanted attention. He began to walk back to the house.

As Jack drew nearer to the property, he noticed an old and unpainted three story barn, set in the back, beyond a line of barren trees. Although there were no lights on, he could hear music coming from the open hayloft door above. It was a slow and melodic song that he knew he'd heard before. After a moment, he recognized it as Leonard Cohen's *Hallelujah*. That's where Bob Woodring had to be.

Rather than walking right up the driveway, Jack decided to cut across the corner of the yard and approach from the edge of the property. With every step that he took, he could feel his heart begin to race faster and faster. He tightly clutched the tire iron in his hand and gave it a few swings, just to get a feel for it. Thunder

155

began to rumble across the evening sky. The storm was quickly approaching.

Jack stopped about fifty feet from the barn and hid himself behind a tree. Realizing that he couldn't just go charging in without a plan, he waited for a few minutes and tried to compose himself. Would he try to talk to Bob first or would he just sneak in and start swinging the moment he saw him? It was pointless for him to consider these two options. Neither would happen. At that very moment, he heard the sound of a handgun cocking behind him and felt the small barrel pressed against the back of his head.

"Toss it," a voice instructed. Jack threw the tire iron across the yard. "Now turn around."

Jack slowly turned to see Bob Woodring standing before him with a pistol in his hand. He didn't know what to say. He was certain that he was now living the final moments of his life. Bob had tried to kill him before and had no reason to spare him now. Much to his astonishment though, Bob lowered the gun and began to chuckle.

"What the F..." Jack began with bewilderment but was cut off. Bob quickly raised the weapon again and began to laugh a bit harder. Jack took a step back and Bob regained his composure. The look on his face changed instantly from amusement to severity. Jack stopped.

"I'm surprised that it took you this long to figure it out," Bob said as his brows furrowed. "Nevertheless, you've been expected."

"How did you know I was here?"

"I could hear you coming a mile away. You really need to get the exhaust fixed on that rice burner that you drive."

"Oh."

"Inside. Now!"

Jack turned and walked toward the barn with Bob following just a pace behind him. He wasn't quite sure where exactly he was going at first, but as he drew closer, he could see a small door. He expected to be shot in the back of the head at any moment but was astounded to find himself still alive when they reached the door.

"Bob?" Jack began.

"Keep going and shut up!" Bob shoved him through the

door and a moment later, Jack found himself inside of a large and open barn. It was quite dark and he half-expected to hear animals of some sort, maybe a horse or some pigs, but there were none. All that he could hear was the Leonard Cohen song playing. Apparently, Bob had it on repeat. "This is good enough," Bob said. "Sit down."

Jack crouched down on the dry earthy floor with his back leaning against a stall. Bob Woodring, his handgun still trained on his captive, crossed the room and turned on the lights.

"So, are you going to kill me?"

"No," Bob replied as he uncocked the hammer, "I'm not going to kill you. Unless you want me to?"

"That's okay. I'll pass."

"So what was it that finally clued you in?" Bob asked as he lowered the gun.

"Mr. Swift's obituary."

"How's that?"

"Archibald Swift. You used to work for him. I've been researching his former property out in Greeley Township. At first I suspected Percy Stuart, but after I found out that he had an alibi for where he was when I was attacked on Saturday night, I decided to take a second look at the previous owners of that house. I saw that Mr. Swift was an undertaker and suddenly remembered you from the morgue. You saw those articles on Pam's desk and knew what I was working on."

"How did you find out about the house in Greeley?"

"My cousin's a psychic."

Bob struck Jack across the face with the barrel of the handgun.

"Stop being funny! Tell me the truth. How did you know?"

Jack grabbed his nose but could tell right away that it wasn't broken. Blood was flowing rather quickly from a deep gash across the bridge. He straightened himself up and glared at Bob.

"I *am* telling the truth. Pam's sister Trish is a psychic and a medium. She guided me to that property late last week."

"It had to be more than that."

"It was. You drove luxury cars. Former funeral vehicles?"

"That's right."

"You also had a chemical smell on you."

"I don't smell like chemicals," Bob told him with a touch of agitation in his voice.

"It was embalming fluid. Wasn't it?"

"Oh yeah," he replied, a slight smile on his face. "The scent really gets me in the mood. I carry a jar of it with me sometimes. What else?"

"There's the flashlight. You probably use it when you're making pick-ups at night or trying to find an address."

"You're good at this."

"What really did it though was the house in Greeley Township. The basement had walls like a prison. I was certain that it was connected. Actually, I'm surprised that the FBI didn't figure it out after the bodies of those two girls were found out there."

"You know about them too?"

"Yeah. But something puzzles me about that. If you work for a funeral home, why bury them? Why not cremate them to destroy the evidence?"

"Are you kidding me? Do you know how hard it is to sneak a corpse, let alone two, into a crematorium?"

"I saw that they were dead since 1985. Why bury them out by your boss' house? Wouldn't he have gotten suspicious?"

"Suspicious? Not a chance. The old man had Alzheimer's and hardly knew what was going on."

"But why there? Why not somewhere else? That's how I was able to make the connection to you. I'd have figured that you'd want to put as much space between those corpses and yourself as possible."

"Not necessarily. Besides, it seemed like a nice place and out of the way of prying eyes."

There was a large crash of thunder. For a moment, Jack thought that Bob had shot him, but realized almost immediately that he was fine. The storm was getting closer.

"So what happened to the others?" continued Jack.

"What others?"

"The other girls that you kidnapped. The ones from around here and Pittsburgh and all the other places."

"Oh, they're sleeping. They're always sleeping. Resting

peacefully in the cradles that I made for them, except for the two that were so rudely woken up from that field in Greeley."

"You mean dead, don't you?"

"Call it what you will," Bob continued nonchalantly.

"Where did you bury them?" Jack asked. Bob began to chuckle again. He crouched down and brought his face rather uncomfortably closer to Jack's.

"I'm not telling," he whispered. "They're mine." Bob stood and took a step back. "They'll always be mine!" he announced. "And not you or anyone else for that matter will ever take them from me!" He pointed the gun at Jack. "Speaking of which," he said in a normal tone as he lowered the gun again, "Who hired you to find me?"

"Hired me?"

"I'm sorry. Do I stu- stu- stu- stutter? Who hired you? I'm certain that you didn't just start looking into past disappearances for the hell of it. Was it that Call bitch?"

"So you knew her?"

"No. I didn't know her."

"So how did you know her name?"

"I read the papers," Bob snorted. "And I make it a point to know the name of the bitch that cost me my hobby. You know? I had to move and start all over again because of her."

"I'm not working for Lauren Call. She's been trying to forget about all of this for many years now."

"And I was so certain that it was her," Bob said with a look of confusion across his face. "Okay then. If not her, who?"

"I'm not saying."

Bob raised the gun again and pointed it directly at Jack's head.

"You tell me!" he shouted.

"Not a chance."

Bob cocked the hammer back.

"Last chance. Tell me or die!"

"I thought you weren't going to kill me."

Bob started to chuckle again. His chuckle soon grew into a maniacal laugh.

"I guess I lied," he said, taking aim.

"Drop your weapon!" a voice shouted. Both Bob and Jack

looked over to see Special Agent Andrew Spurlock standing in the doorway with his firearm drawn. "I said drop it!" he commanded again.

Bob looked back over at Jack and took aim once again. There was a sudden popping sound and Bob went into a spin. He landed on the ground just beside Jack. Jack tried to scramble to his feet, but before he could, was seized around the shoulder by Bob, who now pressed the gun firmly against his right temple.

"Let him go!" Spurlock demanded.

Bob drew Jack in closer and put his mouth up to his ear.

"You won't find them," Bob whispered through bloodied teeth and lips. "They're mine." Jack briefly glanced down at Bob's chest and could see that he was shot pretty close to the heart. "But you must tell me. Who are you working for?"

Jack figured that Bob Woodring would either be dead in a few minutes or would safely be in federal custody and that there would be no harm in telling him now.

"I'm working for Shelby Tomlinson," Jack quietly replied.

An expression of disgust passed over Bob Woodring's face. He looked up at Jack, glanced over at Agent Spurlock and back at Jack again. He began to laugh uncontrollably and shake his head. He slowly pulled the barrel end of the firearm off of Jack's temple.

"I go to them now," Bob declared. He placed the pistol into his own mouth, pulled the trigger and fell back. Bob Woodring was dead.

A moment later, two more federal agents appeared in the doorway. Agent Spurlock came running over to Jack and helped him up.

"Are you alright Mr. Sullivan?"

"I'm fine, and you can call me Jack. I think we're passed formalities."

"Here," Spurlock said as he handed Jack a handkerchief. "Hold this to your nose." Jack obliged.

"How long were you out there?"

"Not long at all. I was at the front door when I heard shouting from back here. I came running over and saw him aiming a gun at your head."

"So you didn't hear any of what he told me?"

"No. What did he say?"

"He…"

"Hold on," Agent Spurlock interrupted as he turned to the other two agents that had just arrived. "Would someone please turn off that damned music?"

The agents spread out to find the source.

"I'm sorry, Jack. Please go on."

"Well, he told me that we'd never find the other girls. That they're his."

"Did he mention Rebecca Lowe?"

"No. We didn't get that far. Even if we did, I don't think he was going to tell me."

Just then, the music stopped and Jack could hear that it was raining outside.

"Thank you!" Agent Spurlock announced. "Well, She has to be around here somewhere," he said as he turned his attention back towards Jack. "The question is where."

The two agents returned.

"There was a CD player in the stall over there," one said.

"That's fine," Spurlock replied. "Look, I want you to spread out and search the place. Rebecca Lowe is probably somewhere in this barn."

The federal agents fanned out and began to call Rebecca's name. Jack stood leaning up against the stall door and continued to wipe the blood from the bridge of his nose.

"Anything?" an agent called out.

"Nothing yet," another replied. "Keep looking!"

Just then, Jack remembered something that Shelby had told him. Something about being held in a basement for two weeks. Rebecca Lowe wasn't in the barn. She was in the house: in the basement.

"She not out here!" Jack called out. The three agents reemerged and looked at him. "She's in the house."

The two agents that had arrived later ran out the door. Agent Spurlock stopped and stared at Jack.

"Are you certain? Did he tell you that?"

"He didn't need to. Come on."

Jack ran out into the pouring rain with Agent Spurlock close behind him. In no time, they arrived at the house where the other two agents were trying to break down the back door.

161

"Can you get it?" Agent Spurlock asked them.

"It must be bolted," one replied.

"Try over here!" Jack yelled as he located a cellar door. The three men came running. It was padlocked. Agent Spurlock kicked at the latch until it gave way and came flying off. They descended the short set of stairs and found themselves in a dark basement with concrete floors. They turned on their flashlights, spread out again and continued to call her name. Jack soon located a small room that seemed to resemble a storage closet. He pulled on the latch and opened it with no trouble at all. There, lying unconscious on the floor and shackled to the wall was a young girl. She looked emaciated and severely beaten from head to toe.

"She's here!" he cried out. The other three came running over. Agent Spurlock ran into the small room and checked the girl for vital signs.

"She's alive." He told them, "but only just." He turned and investigated the area around him. There were surgical needles everywhere. "She must be drugged," he deduced. "Someone call it in."

Chapter 19

"Please try not to squint so much, sir. You're just making it harder."

Jack was lying on a gurney in the back of an ambulance with a bright light shining directly on his face. A paramedic was attempting to stitch his lacerated nose shut, but Jack wasn't making it very easy. He had refused being administered Novocain, as he had developed a tolerance to it many years earlier. As the paramedic put it, they were just going to have to do this "the old fashioned way".

"Are you almost done with him?" Agent Spurlock asked. Jack couldn't see him, but recognized his voice.

"That depends," the medic replied. "If I could get him to hold still for just a few moments, we'd be done."

"Jack, please cooperate with him."

"I hate needles. Can't you guys just tape it shut or something?"

"Sure we can," the medic said, "if you want it to bleed through in ten minutes and end up with a huge scar on your face, plus run a risk of it getting infected."

"Okay. Fine. Just do it."

"Good. Now take a deep breath and hold it."

Jack inhaled and held his breath.

"Quick pinch," the medic continued. There was a short, prickly sensation between Jack's eyes. "Okay, we're almost done. Let me just tie it off..."

"This sucks," complained Jack.

"I'm sure it does," replied the medic as he turned off his light. "And... we're done."

Jack sat up and looked at himself in a mirror that hung on the wall beside him. He viewed the new needlework on his face and grunted.

"Now that wasn't so bad," Agent Spurlock added. Jack leered at him. "Come on. There are a few things I need you to look at."

Jack climbed out of the ambulance. The whole area was awash in red and blue strobe lights. Another ambulance was parked beside the one he had just stepped out of. The back doors were closed and he could only guess that Rebecca Lowe was being treated inside. Next to that sat a hearse with the name Kollifer written on the side. Jack felt quite bad for the driver that had to come and pick up Bob Woodring's body. Aside from losing a co-worker, he must have felt some embarrassment over the fact that this friend was also a serial killer.

Further up the road, close to where he had parked, Jack could see many sets of white floodlights. He was a bit curious as to what was happening over there. Agent Spurlock answered his unasked question.

"It's the media," he said. "We figured it would only have been a matter of time before they showed up. We were hoping to have that hearse and ambulance out of here by the time they did."

"My car's down there somewhere."

"That's right, the black Mazda. I saw it a few minutes ago. It's okay, but is surrounded by reporters right now. They're waiting for a statement."

"What are you going to tell them?"

"Well, we're not releasing any names just yet. We're still waiting for Rebecca Lowe's parents to arrive."

"How is she?"

"Rebecca? She's in pretty bad shape. She's conscious now, but is still quite traumatized by what she's gone through."

"How much of it does she remember?"

"Everything; which is rather unfortunate. It'll probably take her years of therapy to get over. We haven't interviewed her yet and it'll be some time before we do. We did ask her a few questions though and it turns out that you were right."

"Right about what?"

"Fourteen days. She told us that he was going to kill her tonight."

"How did she know?"

"Believe it or not, but the son of a bitch actually told her. Sick jerk probably got off on her reaction too."

"You said there was something you wanted me to see?"

"Yeah, it's back here."

Jack followed Agent Spurlock past the house and into the back yard. They approached the barn and Jack began to slow down. For some reason, he was feeling a bit apprehensive about going back in there. It was a lot like the way he felt when he had visited Pam at the morgue.

"Are you okay?" Agent Spurlock asked.

Jack stopped and looked at the barn for a moment.

"Yeah. I'm fine. It's just... never mind."

He continued to follow the agent into the barn. All of the lights were now turned on and the place didn't seem nearly as big as it did when Jack had been in there earlier. Also, the place was full of police officers and FBI agents. Some were writing down notes, a couple of them were taking photographs and a few were standing in smaller groups talking with one another. As Jack and Agent Spurlock entered, these agents and police officers turned their attentions towards them.

"What's going on?" Jack whispered.

"It's nothing. We're just concluding our investigation."

"Bull. What is it really?"

"Well, maybe they're a bit curious to get a look at the guy who just solved this case."

Jack felt his ego inflate slightly.

"Am I going to be questioned for this?" he asked.

"You already have been, back on Monday when I interviewed you at your apartment. Aside from that, I think we already have just about everything that we're going to need from you."

"That's a relief. What did you want to show me?"

"It's up here."

Jack followed Agent Spurlock up a set of stairs and into the hayloft. Ahead of them was a door. Agent Spurlock walked over and opened it. A dim orange light poured out of the room. Jack cautiously approached, not quite sure of what he was about to see.

"What the hell?"

The walls were plastered entirely with newspaper and magazine articles, photos and crude drawings. There were so many of them that hardly an inch of the original wall color was visible.

"This is what I meant by 'just about everything'."

"I don't get it."

"Well Jack, we don't quite get it either. We think it might

have something to do with his earlier victims. We figured that you had done such a great job in finding this guy that we'd like to invite you to try to make sense out of all of this. From what I can tell, you seem to know more about him than any of us and if anyone can figure this out, I'm sure that you can."

"Wow. I don't know what to say."

"You can say that you'll try."

"Sure. What could it hurt? Has the room been photographed yet?"

"Photographed. Fingerprinted. Documented. Scoured through with a fine-toothed comb. They're already done in here."

"Do you mind if I take a look around for a bit?"

"Not at all. You take as much time as you need. Just let me know when you're done. We're probably going to take all of this with us when we leave."

"Will do."

Jack wandered about the room trying to take in as much as he could. None of it seemed to make any sense to him. There were articles from magazines and newspapers with doodles all over them, a few photographs of women with big scribble marks over their genitals, and large drawings of squares and rectangles with numbers inside of them. Across the room were what appeared to be pages torn out of a book. They all seemed to be from different volumes. If Jack didn't know any better, he'd have thought that these were simply done at random, but knew otherwise.

Up against a wall across the room sat a small writing desk. Jack walked over and browsed its contents. He thought about the desk in his own apartment and wondered in some way if this was Bob Woodring's evil answer to it. For every good thing in the world, there was something wicked that canceled it out: a doppelganger so to speak. It seemed reasonable to Jack that while he was using his desk to stop him, Bob would be using his for his own perverse means.

Jack investigated the desk rather closely. The items that were scattered about the surface seemed to be quite ordinary: much like the items that one would expect to find on anyone's desk. There were a few books, some compact discs, an ashtray and a few empty cans of beer. He figured that the drawers might hold something of greater interest. He started with the center drawer. It had a keyhole, but Jack was quite surprised to find it unlocked. It was just as well. The drawer was completely empty. He opened the others one at a time but found nothing unusual about their contents.

Suddenly, Jack was struck with a thought. He always kept some extra cash secreted away in his apartment, just in case of an emergency. He had an excellent hiding place for it too, that being in a hidden compartment on his desk. Jack opened up the drawers again. This time he reached into the backs and felt around the bottoms looking for a panel that might slide open. He found none. Next, he crouched down onto the floor, climbed under the desk and began to look up at it from a different angle.

"What are you doing?" Agent Spurlock asked.

"Taking a nap."

"What?"

"I'm kidding. I'm just trying to figure something out."

"And what's that?"

"Let you know when I find it."

Jack began to feel his way across the bottom of the desk, but found nothing of interest. He closed his eyes for a moment and a curious thought crossed his mind. He pulled himself out from under the desk and stood up.

"Anything?"

"Nothing," Jack replied. "Quick question though."

"What's that?"

"Did the hearse from Kollifer's leave yet?"

"I don't know. It may have."

"Can you check?"

"Sure." Agent Spurlock pulled out his cell phone, pressed a couple of buttons, stepped out of the room and began to talk. Jack rapped on the desk a few times and listened closely. After a moment, Agent Spurlock returned.

"It's still here," he said. "I told them to hold on for a few more minutes."

"That's great," Jack replied as he walked past him. "Come on."

"Where are you going?"

"Outside."

The two of them came down from the hayloft and exited the barn. In a little over a minute, they were back up by the road again. One of the ambulances had already left but the other, the one that was treating Rebecca Lowe, was still sitting there. Jack could hear excited voices coming from within and assumed that her parents had finally arrived.

Jack continued over to the hearse where the driver was waiting.

"So how can I help you?" the driver asked.

"I need to see Mr. Woodring's possessions: anything that he had on him."

"They're in a box up here. Hold on."

The driver opened the front passenger's side door and retrieved a small plastic bin. He handed it to Jack, who opened it and began to sort through the items. He pushed past the wallet, pack of Kent cigarettes, lighter, pocket change and scraps of paper until he found what he was looking for. He retrieved a set of keys and handed the box back to the driver.

"Thanks," he said and turned back to Agent Spurlock. "Got it. Let's go."

They hurried across the yard and back towards the barn.

"What is that?" Agent Spurlock asked.

"It's a set of keys."

"I can see that, but what do you need those for?"

"I'll show you."

They reentered the barn and ascended the stairs into the hayloft once more. Jack led the way as they walked into the room. He stopped at the desk and turned to face Agent Spurlock.

"I want to show you something."

"And what's that?"

"That things aren't always what they seem to be. Take this desk for example. Did anyone go through it before I did?"

"Of course. We didn't see anything of particular value or interest in it though."

"What about this drawer?" Jack asked as he pointed to the one with the keyhole."

"Yeah, we checked that one too. It's empty. And what did you need the key for? It's unlocked."

"Well, yes and no." Jack pulled the drawer open and

revealed the fact that there was nothing in it. "But watch this." He closed the drawer tightly and inserted an old key into the hole. He turned the latch and there was a clicking sound. He gave the drawer a tug and it was firmly locked.

"Okay," Agent Spurlock interrupted. "So, the lock still works?"

"Hold on." Jack continued to turn the lock until there was another click followed by a sudden thumping sound. "And... Eureka." He pulled open the drawer. It was now quite full of items.

"What the..."

"I give you the vanishing drawer of Bob Woodring," Jack announced with a slight hint of pleasure.

"How in the hell did you figure that out?"

"I just got back from a trip to New York where I had purchased something like this for Claude Dresden. That was the trunk that you had mentioned him taking to his sister's in Toledo. Only that one was full of magic tricks and the like. This one is full of...um." Jack glanced down at the drawer's contents. "Oh my God."

"What?" Agent Spurlock took a step closer and peered into the drawer. "Oh shit. Step back and don't touch anything." He walked over to the door and called down the stairs. "Harris! Get up here quick and bring Jenkins and Novak with you!"

A moment later, three more federal agents had arrived. Agent Spurlock escorted them over to the desk. The four of them huddled around the open drawer discussing its contents. A moment later, one of them pulled out a camera and began to shoot photographs. As he did this, one of the other agent's, a broad shouldered man whom Jack assumed to be Harris, pulled on a pair of surgical green rubber gloves. He reached into the drawer, retrieved the items and set them on the desk. One of these items was a long and rust knife, which he placed into a plastic bag. The agents continued to talk amongst themselves as one of them randomly took pictures. After a moment, Agent Spurlock turned to Jack.

"I hope you have a strong stomach."

"Why's that?" Jack asked.

"Because some of these are pretty bad."

Jack slowly approached the desk. The other agents stepped to the side to let him in. There, sitting on top of the desk, was a series of photographs scattered about. The first ones that he noticed were of young girls either tied up or shackled. He had noticed one of these just after he'd opened the drawer. As he took a closer look, he began to notice that some of the girls in the photographs were dead. When he caught sight of one picture, that of a girl whose face was mutilated beyond recognition, he felt himself grow quite nauseous. He turned and quickly ran for the hayloft door. For a second, Agent Spurlock thought that he was going to jump, but saw instead that he was vomiting. Jack hadn't eaten anything all day and was only bringing up stomach bile. He placed an arm around Jack's shoulder.

"It'll be alright," he said. "I told you that some of them were pretty bad. Can I get you anything? A bottle of water perhaps?" Jack nodded. "Novak. Please go and fetch a bottle of water for Mr. Sullivan here."

Jack straightened himself out, spit once again out the hayloft door and wiped his mouth on the sleeve of his sweater.

"How many photos are there?" he asked Agent Spurlock.

"Close to thirty by the looks of it."

"Does each photo contain a different girl?"

"How do you mean?"

"Is the same girl pictured in more than one photograph?"

"Oh. It's hard to say, really. Some of them have hoods or pillowcases or something over their heads."

"Do me a favor and pull the worst of them to the side. I can't look at them."

"Harris?" Agent Spurlock called over.

"Got it." The brawny agent began to pick up some of the photos and set them in a stack to the side with their faces down.

"Okay, come on." Agent Spurlock escorted Jack back over to the desk. Agent Novak was there waiting with a bottle of water. He handed it to Jack, who opened it and took a deep swig.

"Thanks," he said as he set the bottle down. He looked over the photos once more. Agent Spurlock was slightly off in his count. Even with the most grotesque snapshots pulled to the side, there were still close to forty on the desk. "There's a lot more here than I first guessed."

"How's that?" Agent Spurlock asked.

"Victims. There are more victims here than I thought."

"How many were you aware of?"

"Somewhere around twenty."

Jack gazed at the faces in the pictures. They were filled with such terror that again, Jack found it hard to keep his composure. A few of the faces he recognized from the articles, such as Nadine Somerset, but most he couldn't place. One face he knew as soon as he saw it. The severely beaten girl was wearing a denim jacket covered with colorful marker drawings. It was her bright blue eyes though that gave her away. The photo was that of a 14-year-old Shelby Tomlinson. Jack could feel tears welling up. He fought them back as best he could.

"What is it?" Agent Spurlock asked.

"Nothing," Jack replied. "I'm okay."

"Are you sure?"

"Yeah... I'm sure."

"Do you recognize any of them?"

"A few. I'll give you copies of the articles that I have. You should be able to make a match with some of them."

"Thanks. We really appreciate it."

"It's no problem. Could you do me a favor though?"

"Anything."

Could you give me copies of the pictures that you took of the walls in this room? I'm sure that Bob Woodring wouldn't have hung all of this up at random."

"So you think there's a pattern to this stuff?"

"I'm not certain, but it was something that he said to me earlier that has me thinking."

"What was that?"

"He mentioned this as being his hobby."

"That's a pretty disturbing thought."

"I know, but occasionally when someone gets wrapped up in something that they consider a hobby, they let to let it consume them. I get the same way when I'm writing or working on a long research project. I think that there might be something here on these walls."

"You've got it, Jack. I'll drop by tomorrow morning with the photos and you can give me copies of those articles."

Jack checked the time on his cell phone. It was nearly eleven. If Shelby were coming over that evening, he'd certainly have missed her by now.

"I'm going home then. Is there any chance of getting past the media without them bothering me?"

"Yeah, we're about due to release our statement anyway. While I'm talking to the press, you can get to your car and leave."

"Thanks. Can you do me one other favor?"

"Sure."

"Can you not mention my name to the media?"

"I can withhold your name if you wish Jack, but it's all over with and I think we should give credit where credit's due."

"Well, just don't tell them for now. Maybe you could wait a few days for the buzz to die down some. The last thing I want is a media frenzy on my front porch."

"I understand."

The federal agents escorted Jack up to the front of the property. Jack made sure to pick up his tire iron from where he had tossed it earlier that evening. Agent Spurlock and a few other agents walked over to where the press had been patiently waiting behind the yellow police ribbon and began to speak. It was a good ploy on his part. The statement was being made just as the eleven o'clock news was starting. Jack nonchalantly walked over to his car. As he opened the door, he could hear Special Agent Spurlock addressing the reporters.

"And thanks to the actions of a proactive citizen, who wishes to remain anonymous at this time, we were able to…"

Jack got into his car, turned over the ignition and pulled away. Only a couple of people noticed the black Mazda Protegé 5 as it drove off into the stormy night.

Chapter 20

Jack woke to a gray and blustery morning. Strong winds from the north beat sporadic drops of rain against his windows. It was a stark contrast from the beautiful weather of the last few days. Indian Summer had come to an end. The first thought that crossed Jack's mind was of going out for a hot cup of coffee. He'd definitely be wearing a sweater and, quite possibly, a pair of long johns as well. Just by glancing at that cold and steely sky, he could tell that it was going to be a damp, bone-chilling day.

He climbed out of bed, threw on his robe and walked out into the living room where he turned on the television. The local news was just beginning. He sat on the couch and decided that he'd catch the headlines before taking a shower. The lead story came on with a "Breaking News" graphic that included ominous lettering and dramatic music.

"And we have breaking news coming in this morning out of Parkington, where a missing 12-year-old North Coventry girl has been found alive," the anchor boldly stated. "We go now live to beat reporter Nancy O'Neil who picks up the story there. Nancy, what can you tell us about the events that transpired there last night?"

"Well, Jim," the reporter began, "It's not too often that a story like this is given a happy ending, but a happy ending is what we have here today. If you'll look behind me, you'll see the house where, according to authorities, 12-year-old Rebecca Lowe had been held for the last two weeks by this man, 57-year-old Robert Marshall Woodring." A picture of Bob, possibly from his driver's license, was flashed on the screen. "If you'll remember, we first brought you the story back on October 18th of how Rebecca Lowe had vanished while walking home from a friend's house the night before. A massive search was conducted, but nothing turned up. Then, last night, following a tip from an anonymous source, federal agents were called out to this residence on Weymouth Road and it was here that Miss Lowe was discovered in the basement. Details are still coming in at this hour regarding the circumstances that surround her rescue, but what is known is that Robert Woodring, the alleged kidnapper, was shot and killed in an exchange of gunfire with federal agents. What is also known is that the anonymous tipster was on the premises at the time of this exchange and that he or she played an important roll in rescuing Rebecca Lowe and tracking down her abductor."

"And has there been any word on Rebecca Lowe's condition?" the anchor asked.

"From what we know Jim, she was initially taken to Seneca Hospital and from there was transported to the trauma unit at Mount Hope Medical Center. Her condition is not known at this hour as we're still awaiting word from hospital officials."

"We're also hearing word that the alleged kidnapper may have been involved in a number of other missing children's cases. Has there been any confirmation of this?"

"No Jim. When asked, federal investigators refused to comment on any other cases that the alleged kidnapper may or may not have been involved in. They did tell us though that they will be issuing another statement later on this afternoon, detailing more of this case and the events that led up to the rescue of Rebecca Lowe."

"We look forward to that. Nancy O'Neil reporting from Parkington. Thank you, Nancy."

"Thank you, Jim."

"And remember to keep it tuned here for breaking news regarding this story and we'll bring you the latest details as they come in. You can also visit our website for constant updates. In other news, last night's storms wreaked havoc across the region, causing power outages and significant wind damage. We turn it over to Chief Meteorologist Kevin Court for details. Kevin?"

Jack turned off the television. He was glad to see that Agent Spurlock hadn't given out his name. He walked over to the front window and peered outside just to make sure there weren't any camera crews or reporters in his front yard. To his relief, there were none. He walked into the bathroom, dropped his robe, shaved and took a shower.

When he had finished, Jack donned a pair of thermal underwear, denim jeans and a turtleneck sweater. He grabbed his patchwork hat and distressed leather jacket and was out the door. As he raced up to the gas station for a cup of coffee, he decided to turn on the radio. The first station he came across had a local talk radio program on. The topic of discussion was the events that had unfolded out in Parkington the night before. Jack was surprised to see this story getting so much attention. Apparently, it was much bigger than he had first thought.

He walked into the gas station, poured himself a tall cup of dark-roasted coffee, added some hazelnut creamer and picked up a couple of giant chocolate chunk cookies. Jack was anything but a healthy eater, especially in the morning. As he went to pay for it at the counter, he glanced down to his left and saw the front page of The Plain Dealer. The headline read: "*12-Year-Old Girl Rescued From House Of Horrors.*" He couldn't believe how fast the media had picked up on this story.

He got back into the car and turned the radio back on. The national news was just starting. It wasn't the lead story, but the rescue of Rebecca Lowe had still managed to make its way into the national spotlight.

After returning to his house, Jack booted up his laptop and jumped online. There were quite a few emails waiting for him. Most were spam, but one was from his cousin Trish.

> *Jack,*
> *I saw the news this morning and can't help but wonder who that anonymous tipster was that lead the FBI to Rebecca Lowe. Pam called and told me all about your conversation with her yesterday. I was sorry to hear that the kidnapper was an acquaintance of hers but am relieved that you found the right guy.*
> *We were pretty busy here last night, as we had a couple of groups in for an overnight ghost hunt, but our schedule is clear for the next two weeks. I'm thinking about coming up tomorrow evening. I know that I was just there, but I have a feeling that I need to come anyway. I don't know what it is just yet, but I think it has something to do with the case you've been working. I'll give you a call when I get into town.*
> *With love,*
> *Trish*

Jack was extremely curious about Trish's email. The case was over, yet she seemed to feel that there was still more to it. What that might be, he had no idea. Perhaps it had something to do with the photos of the room that Agent Spurlock was supposed to be dropping off that morning, Jack thought. He looked over at the clock and saw that it was already close to eleven. The morning was nearly over.

As Jack waited patiently for Agent Spurlock's arrival, he continued to check the rest of his emails and printed out the articles that Shelby had sent him a little over a week earlier. After about a half an hour, an email came up from Corley, his downstairs neighbor.

> *Hey,*
> *I'm heading up to the Great Lakes Brewing Company this afternoon. It's the annual first tapping of their Christmas Ale. Thought you might want to come with. Drop me a line after while and let me know.*
> *Corley*

Jack had totally forgotten about that. It was a yearly tradition that he and Corley would get together with a few of their friends and sample that season's holiday brew. The recipe varied slightly from year to year and seemed to get better each time. Jack fired back a brief message telling Corley that he'd be happy to join her and to call when she was heading up. Just as he sent this message, the doorbell rang. Jack jumped up from his desk, ran down the stairs and threw open the door. Agent Spurlock was standing out on the front porch holding a brown file folder in his hands. He jogged down the next set of stairs and opened the front door.

"Good morning Agent Spurlock," Jack greeted.

"Good morning. And you can call me Drew. Like you said before. We're past formalities."

"Thanks, Drew. Come on up."

The agent followed Jack into his apartment and took a seat on the couch. Fionn, Jack's yellow cat, jumped up on his lap and began to rub his face on him.

"Oh, sorry about that," Jack said as he scooped up the cat and put him on the floor.

"That's okay. I normally wouldn't mind so much, but I'm slightly allergic to cats. We have one at my house, but she stays in the back room."

"You married?"

"Yeah for about eight years now. It's my wife's cat, but she wouldn't part with her for the world. I'm fine as long as I don't have close contact with it."

"Any children?"

"Yeah. We have a 6-year-old son named Aiden. He just started kindergarten this year. What about you, Jack? I know you're not married, but do you have any kids?"

"No. Plenty of nieces and nephews though, the oldest of which is in high school now. Oh, I have those articles for you."

Jack crossed the room and pulled the stack of articles from the tray on his printer. He walked back over to the couch and handed them to Agent Spurlock, who began at once to leaf through them.

"Looks like you have quite a lot here."

"Like I said, I thought there were somewhere around twenty separate cases. Based off of those photographs that we found last night..."

"That *you* found last night," Agent Spurlock corrected. "Credit where credit's due. Remember?"

"Okay. Based off of the photographs that *I* found last night, there seems to be many more cases than I've just handed you. I hope that you can make a match to some of them."

"Speaking of which," the agent said as he reached for the brown file folder, "I have those photographs of the items hanging on the walls of that room." He opened the file folder and handed Jack a short stack of photos. "I just hope that you can make more sense out of it than any of us were able to."

"So you've had someone else analyze these?"

"Quite a few people actually. We were looking for codes and encryption. We have a number of people on our staff that specialize in that field."

"And they weren't able to come up with anything?"

"Oh sure, they were able to come up with something."

177

"Really? What was that?"

"That it's not a code at all. Or at least I should say that it's not one that they could figure out."

"Oh." Jack felt a bit disappointed with this. He always loved a good riddle or puzzle.

"At first, they thought it was an Ottendorf cipher."

"A what?"

"A substitution cypher."

"I still don't follow."

Agent Spurlock took the pictures from Jack and flipped ahead to a few close-up photos of the walls.

"Well, if you look here, we have these squares drawn out on pieces of paper. There are numbers written inside a few of the smaller ones. The larger squares, for the most part, don't have any numbers in them at all."

"Go on."

"Well," Agent Spurlock continued as he flipped ahead to a few more photos. "If you look on this wall over by the door, we have a bunch of pages torn out of books. A substitution cipher takes a series of numbers and replaces them with letters from a corresponding book or page to spell out a word or a message. For example: the numbers 8 and 15 would mean eighth line, fifteenth letter. Say that would be the letter 'J'. You write it in beside the numbers. Keep doing this until you've spelled out the entire message."

"Yeah, I remember seeing these pages on the wall last night. You thought it was a code?"

"At first. The problem they ran into is that there is no key or index to decode the message. We tried using every line of every page, forward and back, and still couldn't come up with anything."

"So then maybe they're right. Maybe it isn't a code at all."

"Well, if it isn't a code, what is it?"

Jack picked up one of the photographs that contained the images of the pages hanging on the wall.

"Do you know what books these pages came from?" he asked.

"Yeah. For the most part, they came from trashy romance novels."

"Which parts?"

"The more erotic chapters, I believe."

"Hmm. Maybe these don't have anything to do with the other items on the walls. Maybe they have something to do with his character."

"What do you mean?"

"Well look at it like this. He feels sexually repressed and isolated. Maybe these pages are part of a fantasy that he was trying to live out. We know that he sexually assaulted these girls before he killed them. Maybe this was what fueled his actions."

"That's a grim thought. I read a few of the pages and there was some pretty graphic material on them."

"I don't like to think about it either."

"Okay, well, if it's not a code, what's the purpose of these squares with the numbers written in them?"

"Honestly, I don't know. That's something that I'm going to have to figure out."

"Jack, I'm going to leave these photos with you. They're not the originals, but nonetheless, try not to damage them. I also don't have to tell you not to share them with anyone else."

"Of course."

"Well, I have to get back to the office. There's a lot of work ahead of me if I'm going to try to make some matches between these articles and the girls from the photos."

"Looks like there's going to be a lot of work ahead for the both of us. I'll call you the second I figure something out."

"Okay, Jack. You have a good afternoon."

"Thanks, Drew. You too."

With that, Agent Spurlock left Jack's apartment. Jack glanced down at the stack of photos that he had left for him. There was quite a lot to do. A moment later, Jack's phone began to ring. He looked at the caller ID and saw that it was Corley.

"Hello?" he answered.

"Hey Jack. I'm heading up to the brewery. Do you still want to come?"

Jack debated this in his mind for a moment. He had a considerable amount of work to do, but figured that maybe by stepping away from it for a short time, he might be able to get some fresh ideas.

"Sure," he told his downstairs neighbor. "I'll be down in a

second."

He hung up the phone, grabbed his hat and jacket from the newel post and was downstairs in no time. Corley stepped out through the side door and jumped back at the sight of the stitches on the bridge of Jack's nose.

"What the hell happened to you?" she asked.

"Oh, the stitches?"

"Yeah."

"It's nothing."

"Nothing, my ass. It's that case you're on, right?"

"Well, the case is kind of wrapped up now."

There was a pause as Corley was slowly putting two and two together.

"Wait a minute. You said that it was a missing person's case. It wasn't that girl that they found last night out in Parkington, was it?"

"Look. I'd really appreciate it if you didn't tell anyone about this."

"That was you. The anonymous tipster. What happened?"

"I kind of got pistol whipped across the face."

"You've got to tell me all about it."

Jack considered it for a moment.

"Fine, but it stays between us. You can't repeat any of it."

"I promise."

"Good. Hop in and I'll fill you in on the way, but after we get there, not a single mention of it to anyone."

Corley nodded and they got into Jack's car. He shared with her every little detail of the case and all that he had been through since coming back from New York. By the time they reached the Great Lakes Brewing Company, Jack had finished telling his story. They parked the car, walked into the pub and ordered a round of Christmas Ale. After a while, more of their friends began to converge on the brewery for the annual first tapping of the holiday brew. Everyone was curious to know what Jack had done to his nose. His cover story was that he'd slipped while getting out of the tub and had cracked it on the sink. Corley was as good as her word and the Christmas Ale that they were all enjoying. She never once mentioned the case.

Chapter 21

As Jack and Corley left the Great Lakes Brewing Company, everyone wished them well and expressed their anticipation of the Halloween party that was set to occur the following night. The drive back to Hathaway Avenue passed in relative silence. Perhaps it was that Corley was a bit standoffish and didn't know what to say to Jack in regards to the ordeal he had just gone through. Or maybe she was ticked off that he had put the house in jeopardy by taking on such a dangerous case. When they pulled up to the house, Jack learned immediately why Corley was so quiet. As soon as she opened the door, she leaned out and threw up five glasses worth of Christmas Ale. Jack realized it was a good thing that he was driving. Had Corley driven up there, they would have had to take a taxi home, and Corley would have needed to find a way to get back to her car later.

Jack helped his inebriated neighbor into her apartment and laid her out on the couch. He went into the bathroom, retrieved the wastebasket and placed it next to Corley's head. He was a bit bewildered at her intoxication. She was notorious for being able to hold her liquor, but then, it was Christmas Ale: 7.5% alcohol by volume. After making sure that she was comfortable, Jack took the back stairs up to his apartment.

It was getting late; well after nine at night. Jack sat on the couch in his apartment looking over the photos that Agent Spurlock had dropped off earlier. Some of the items that Bob Woodring had hung on the wall were starting to make sense. The pages torn from the romance novels seemed to be a tome that spelled out all of his desires. Jack looked closer at the pictures of the women from the many different magazines. They all seemed to have pen marks over their genital regions. At first, Jack thought that Bob was drawing massive amounts of pubic hair on them, but then he had another idea. Maybe he was trying to scribble out these areas. It would make sense that he would. Bob Woodring was attracted to younger girls that might not have any pubic hair at all. Maybe this was his way of taking out his frustrations over that issue.

Jack moved on to a photograph of a set of magazine articles. Their content didn't seem all that interesting, but there were passages written into the margins and what looked like correction scrawled in between the lines. Jack took a closer look. It seemed that every time the article had mentioned a woman by name, Bob had crossed it out and had written in words like *Bitch*, *Cunt* and *Whore*. It went without saying that he had some real issues with women. As Jack investigated the passages written into the margins, he could see that they were variations on the articles next to them. Bob was telling the same story, but from a different point of view. Also, the endings were quite different, usually concluding with someone getting their face torn off. He glanced through a few more of these. It was pretty much the same with each one.

He continued to flip through the photographs. Soon, he came across something that he hadn't noticed the night before. Bob had hung up a series of pictures of different houses. There were eight in all. Jack scanned his eyes across the image and soon found a house that he had expected to see. One of them was of the Rainey House in Greeley Township. As for the other seven, he didn't recognize them at all. They must have been the houses in the other cities that he had taken these girls to. He looked at the photos that immediately followed. They were close-ups of these houses, yet there was nothing written on them to denote where they were located. He could only hope that they would eventually lead him to the other missing girls.

He now went back to the photographs of the squares that were drawn out on paper. He puzzled over it for quite some time but still couldn't come up with an explanation for the numbers. Perhaps it was a code, Jack thought, but they just needed to find the key. He sat back and contemplated where Bob might have hidden this, if one in fact existed. Just then, his doorbell rang. Jack looked up at the clock and saw that it was a little before eleven. He got up from the couch and went down to answer the door. It was Shelby.

"I missed you last night," she said as he opened the door for her.

"Well, I was a little busy."

"I know. It was all over the news today. Oh my God!" she

exclaimed as she noticed his stitches. "What happened to your nose?"

"Oh, I got whacked in the face with a gun."

"I'm so sorry."

"It's nothing," he assured her. "And what are you apologizing for? You didn't do this to me."

"I know, but you got hurt again, and it's because of me."

"Nonsense. Come on up."

They walked up the stairs and into Jack's apartment where Shelby took a seat on the couch.

"So is he really dead?" Shelby asked.

"Yeah. He's dead. But between you and me, he wasn't killed by a federal agent."

"Who then?"

"Well, he took his own life."

"Oh."

"He did confess to killing the others though."

"Did he say what he did with them?"

"Not in so many words. He said that they were 'resting' in cradles that he'd made for them. I'm assuming that means that he buried them. The question is where."

"What are these?" Shelby asked as she reached for the stack of photos.

"Oh." Jack quickly picked them up and carried them over to his desk. "I don't think you want to see those."

Shelby followed him.

"Why not? What are they?"

Jack considered not telling her. Agent Spurlock had asked that he not share them with anyone. He was certain that this also included Shelby. Still, she was his client and he didn't see any harm in at least telling her what they were.

"Alright, they're photos that were taken from Bob Woodring's barn."

"Photos of what?"

"Well, he had a number of things plastered to the walls in one of the rooms. The FBI thinks that I may be able to help them figure out what it all means."

"Have you had any luck?"

"Some, but I'm stumped on one or two things."

"Well, let me have a look. I might be able to help you."

"I can't. I was asked not to share them with anyone. Normally I would show you, but I gave my word."

"There may be something in there that could jog my memory of something."

"I know. I thought about that too. But until I'm told otherwise, I'm afraid that I can't share them."

"Can you at least describe them?"

Jack thought about it for a moment.

"I guess I can't see the harm in that."

They walked back over to the couch and took a seat.

"So what are you stumped on?"

"Well, I've pretty much figured out everything except for some drawings that he had hanging on the wall."

"Okay. What were they drawings of?"

"It's hard to say really. It looks like a cluster of different sized boxes. Some of them have numbers in them and some of them don't."

"A code?"

"That's what the FBI initially thought, but it doesn't seem to be."

"It would really help if I could see these drawings."

"I know, but until I'm told otherwise, I can't show you."

"Okay," Shelby said with a touch of disappointment in her voice, "What else were you stuck on?"

"Well, it's not so much that I'm stuck on it, just a bit baffled is all."

"What is it?"

"He had some pictures of some houses hanging on his walls. One of them was of the Rainey House."

"How many pictures did he have?"

"Eight. I've kind of figured this one out though."

"And what conclusion did you come to?"

"My best guess is that these are the houses that he took these girls to."

"So you think that he used multiple houses in each city?"

"Not exactly. What I think is that he abducted girls from eight different cities."

"How can that be? I was certain that I'd successfully

184

tracked him down from city to city."

"Well, there were two from Buffalo that you didn't know about."

"Buffalo?"

"Yeah, that's where those two girls that were found out in Greeley Township were originally from. There's something else and I've been considering not telling you about this, but I don't see how I can't."

"What is it?"

Jack tried to find the best way to approach this topic.

"While we were going through this room in Bob Woodring's barn, I stopped to check out his desk and found a secret compartment."

"Okay, what was in it?"

Jack hesitated a moment, but then went on.

"It contained somewhere around forty photos of different girls."

"Oh." Shelby was at a loss for words.

"Some of them were alive... and some were not. Some were so graphic that I couldn't even stand to look at them."

"I see."

"No, Shelby, there's more. And I think you need to know this."

"Know what?"

"That *you* were in one of those photos."

"Are you sure?"

"Yes. I'm very sure. Do you remember someone taking your picture at any time?"

Shelby closed her eyes tightly as if trying to recall.

"No," she said. She opened her eyes and gazed at him. "I don't want to think about this anymore."

"Okay, lets talk about something else."

"Even better, let's not talk about anything."

She scooted over towards Jack, threw her arms around him and rested her face against his chest. Jack began to feel drowsy. It had been a long day and he was starting to feel weary from the after affects of the Christmas Ale. He rested his face on the top of her head and was asleep in no time.

Chapter 22

Jack awoke to find himself alone once again. Shelby had left him in the middle of the night, just as she always had. Jack considered himself to be a light sleeper and figured that he would stir at least a little as she got up to leave. As it was, he'd slept soundly through the night. He hoped that maybe some morning he'd wake up and she'd still be there. How nice, he thought, that would be.

He sat up on the couch and looked at the clock. It was well after eleven in the morning. He'd overslept again. He stood up, stretched and peered out the window. Clouds rolled above in different tones of slate gray. It was going to be a day just like the last: cold and damp. Suddenly, Jack remembered that he was set to have his Halloween party that evening. He took a good look at his place. It was something of a mess. The dishes were piling up in the sink, there were food crumbs on the kitchen floor and the cat boxes needed to be cleaned again. He had quite a task ahead of him. He started by shaving and taking a shower.

After getting himself dressed, he drove up to the gas station for a cup of coffee. When he got back home, he sat down on the couch and watched the morning news. The third story was an update on the Rebecca Lowe case. They played the statement that had been made by Agent Spurlock on Wednesday night and retold the circumstances surrounding the death of Bob Woodring and the rescue of Rebecca Lowe, whose condition was listed as *good*. Furthermore, she was to be released from the hospital later that day. Jack was glad to hear this. He was also glad to see that his name hadn't yet made it into the hands of the media. After catching the weather, which told him that it was going to continue to be cold throughout the weekend, Jack turned off the television and set himself to the task of cleaning his apartment.

He loaded the dishwasher, added detergent and turned it on. There, he thought, one less thing to worry about. He next moved on to the carpets. He sprinkled deodorizer, or floor spice as he called it, about the place and let it sit for about fifteen minutes. While he waited, he sipped on his coffee and put on a CD by Westside Steve, an old friend and one of his favorite musicians from Put-In-Bay. He looked out the window, saw that it had started to rain and began to miss the summer and the warm days he'd spent out at the islands. Every other year, he and his friends would go camping for a weekend at South Bass Island State Park. In the evenings, they would catch a cab into town, bar hop along Delaware Avenue and take in the music and atmosphere of that fine island. The Sunday morning trip back to the mainland on the ferry was usually quite rough, but looking back, it was well worth it.

After vacuuming up the floor spice, along with a considerable amount of cat fur, Jack began to wipe down the tables and chairs. As he got over towards his desk, he noticed a small note sitting on the brown file folder that contained the photos from Bob Woodring's barn. He picked it up and read it.

Jack,

I know that you asked me not to, but I looked at these pictures anyway. To be honest, I couldn't make heads or tails out of any of it. After I put them back though, I suddenly remembered something from the night that I escaped. I was waking up in a deep pit that was lined with sticks. I crawled out and ran as fast as I could. I remember that I looked behind me to see if I was being followed, but I wasn't. You had asked if I was taken out to the barn. I told you that I wasn't, that I had walked right past it. I remember now where I was. It was a small wooden shed of some sort. I don't know if this will help you at all and I also hope that you aren't too angry with me for looking at these pictures. I'll stop by later this afternoon. Hope to see you then.

Shelby

Jack was a little miffed that she had gone against something that he had asked her not to do, but there was no point in continuing to be angry. He sat down and read over the note again.

"A deep pit that was lined with sticks," he said to himself. That seemed very odd. Why would she be waking up in a place

187

like that, he wondered. He closed his eyes and tried to picture what that would look like. The first thought that came to him was that she was in some kind of a cage. That didn't make any sense though. She had told him that she'd been kept in the basement. Why would she be moved to a cage out in another building? She had also said in her note that she'd crawled out of this pit; therefore, it had no sticks on top. Another image came to Jack. It was that of a baby lying in a crib.

Something snapped in his mind just then. It was something that Bob Woodring had said to him on Wednesday night. He couldn't remember it verbatim, but it was something about the missing girls being asleep. Then it struck him and the words came out as though Bob Woodring himself was standing right there.

"They're always sleeping. Resting peacefully in the cradles that I made for them."

That was it. Shelby was lying in a cradle in the ground: a cradle that was about to become her grave. He suddenly remembered that the two girls that had been found near that pasture were also lying in pits that were lined with sticks. A chill ran up his spine.

Jack looked back at the note and read on. She had mentioned walking past the barn and running from a wooden shed of some sort. Everything began to fall into place.

Jack opened up the brown file folder and began to flip through the pictures. He soon came to the ones of the drawings of the boxes. As he browsed each one, he looked at the numbers that were written down. The first page had a "2". The next had a "5". The following one had a "3". In almost every case, the number was written down inside of a box. There was one exception. It was a number "2" that was written down next to a long black line. There was also a box, but it was clear on the other side of the page. These weren't part of a code. They were the number of bodies that were buried in a location. The number "2" that was drawn beside the long black line must have indicated the two girls from Buffalo that Bob had buried on the edge of that pasture back in 1985.

Jack looked at the other pages. The boxes, he figured, must have represented houses or buildings on a property. These pages were maps. There were all sorts of numbers scattered about. He added them up. The final body count tally was 39. He found it so hard to believe that someone could kill this many people before getting caught.

Shelby had written that she was running away from a wooden shed. Jack thought about it for a moment. He suddenly remembered his conversation with Percy Stuart. When asked about the property, Mr. Stuart had told him that there was a barn on the property. Shelby had remembered that. He also said that there was a two-story carriage house and an outbuilding of some sort. The carriage house would look nothing like a wooden shed, but an outbuilding certainly would.

Jack had no idea what the property layout for the Rainey House had looked like. He glanced through the photos again and tried to make a match with the number of girls that were missing from the Cleveland area. Strangely, he could find no match. One thing that he did notice about these drawings was that Bob always buried these girls in the same location. There were no multiple burial places on one page. If he had planned to bury Shelby in the outbuilding, then it was a good bet that this was where he had buried the others.

Unfortunately, the Rainey House was long gone and a housing development now occupied the site. This was going to make it harder to find them. Jack would need to begin by finding the property layout for the Rainey House. He thought about it for a moment. He'd done research like this in the past. It meant a trip downtown to the Cleveland Public Library.

It was nearly three in the afternoon as Jack tried to fight his way through the traffic to get downtown. The volume was unusually heavy for that hour, but then Jack remembered that it was Friday and that people were getting out of work early. He was surprised to find a parking spot so close to the library entrance. He wouldn't have to circle the block at all. He jumped out of the car, fed the meter and entered the Stokes Wing of the library. He crossed the lobby, made his way over to the elevators and found one waiting for him. He pressed *six* and was on his way up to the Map Collection.

He entered through the glass doors and set his jacket on the back of a chair at one of the microfilm viewers. Knowing exactly what he was looking for, Jack walked over to a filing cabinet and

189

retrieved a roll of microfilm marked *Sanborn Fire Insurance Maps 1973: A – H*. He walked back over to the viewer, loaded it and began to zip through the images. He stopped at the section on Greeley Township and looked over the index page. He located Indianola Road and scrolled ahead to page 34. There before him sat a layout of the area where the Rainey House once sat. When this map was made, it was still there. Jack looked over the property layout. There he saw the main house, indicated by a heavy outline and dimensions. The map went on to say that the house was made of stone. Just behind this and to the northwest sat the barn. Next to that was the carriage house that Mr. Stuart had mentioned and finally, at the back of the property near the woods, was an outbuilding.

That had to be it. Jack printed out the image and gave it a good look. There were dimensions for the property and all the buildings that sat upon it. He would now have to determine where exactly this location was today. Any trace of the Rainey House and the buildings that accompanied it were long gone.

He walked over to the Realty Atlas Tax Maps for Cuyahoga County. Within a few seconds, he located the one for Greeley Township and flipped ahead to the section containing Indianola Road. As expected, Fleur-de-lis Estates now occupied much of the area. He held up the Sanborn Map of the Rainey property and compared it to the Tax Map. This would take some time. He went over to the photocopier and copied the page. At this, he laid the Sanborn map on top of the printed image. The scale was almost exact, which would make this considerably easier. According to the Tax Map, the spot where the outbuilding had once stood was now a back yard. The question was who's. Jack looked at the Permanent Parcel Number that was written there. He'd have to cross-reference this with the Cuyahoga County Auditor's website when he got home.

The traffic was even worse trying to leave downtown Cleveland. It was sheer gridlock leading up Lakeside Avenue to the entrance ramp of the West Shoreway. Jack tuned in the radio and after a few minutes caught the traffic report. According to the announcer, there was a three-car wreck about a mile ahead at the Westinghouse Curve. He needed to find another route. He hung a

190

left at West Sixth Street and drove up to Superior where he crossed the bridge to the West Side. He'd have to take the surface streets the whole way home.

Jack arrived back at his apartment shortly after four-thirty. He raced up the stairs and threw his jacket and cap on the newel post. He crossed the room, booted up his laptop and connected with the county auditor's website. Quickly, he glanced down at the Permanent Parcel Number that was written on the Tax Map, typed it into the search field and hit *enter*. He wasn't the least bit surprised when it brought up Laverne Quinstead as the property owner.

Immediately, he pulled out the Sanborn Map and checked the measurements in relation to where Mrs. Quinstead's house now stood. From what he was able to tell, the outbuilding had stood about ten feet from the back of her house. He picked up Agent Spurlock's card from his desk and proceeded to call him.

"Spurlock," the agent answered.

"Drew? It's Jack."

"Hi Jack. How can I help you?"

"I figured out what those numbers mean."

"You did. Are you sure?"

"Absolutely."

"Okay, what do they mean?"

"They're graves. They tell how many corpses are buried in one location."

"What?"

"Yeah, it took a while, but I'm certain of it."

"So what do the boxes mean?" Agent Spurlock asked.

"They're buildings. The larger ones are houses and the smaller ones, the ones that contain the numbers, are sheds and barns and the like."

"How did you figure all of this out?"

"It's a long story. Look, the important thing is that I've figured out where he's buried the girls that are missing from the Cleveland area. They're about ten feet off the back of a house, in Fleur-de-lis Estates, that's owned by a woman named Laverne Quinstead."

"Hang on a second. Let me get a pen." There was a moment's pause before Drew Spurlock returned. "Okay, you said

191

that it was in Fleur-de-lis Estates?"

"Yeah. In Greeley Township."

"And the name was Quinstead?"

"That's right. Laverne Quinstead. The spot you'll want to check is about ten feet from the back of her house."

"Okay Jack. Normally I wouldn't do this without more verification, but you've proven yourself more than enough. We'll get a team out there at once."

"Thanks, Drew."

"I'll call and let you know if we find anything."

"I appreciate it."

Jack hung up the phone. There was nothing more for him to do but wait.

Chapter 23

Jack made the calls and postponed his Halloween party. He had a feeling that he would be getting a call from Agent Spurlock at any time. Most were pretty upset, but Jack assured them that it was only being put off for a day. Rick had just picked up a couple of six packs of Christmas Ale, but wouldn't guarantee Jack that he'd still have them by Saturday night.

It was now going on seven and there was still no word. Jack sat down at his laptop and began to pass the time by checking his email. There wasn't much on there, just a few postings on his social networking page. He'd had enough. He turned off the laptop, walked over to the couch and turned on the television. A moment later, his phone rang. It was Trish.

"Jack?"

"Hi Trish. Are you back in town?"

"Just about. I'm on my way over to your place."

"Really?"

"Yeah. There are a few things that I need to show you."

"What is it?" His curiosity was piqued.

"I'd rather wait until I see you."

"Oh. Okay."

"I should be there in about ten minutes or so."

"That soon?" Jack looked about him. He had started to clean the apartment, but still hadn't quite finished.

"Is that okay?"

"Sure. I just need to straighten up a bit."

"Oh, don't make a fuss over me."

"It's okay. It'll just take me a moment. I'll see you in a few."

Jack hung up the phone and took another look at his place. He quickly grabbed the wastebasket from the bathroom and cleaned out the litter boxes. Next, he finished wiping down the chairs. Finally, he swept up the kitchen floor and dumped the dustpan into the kitchen wastebasket. He removed the garbage bag, tied it off, took it down the stairs and carried it out to the garbage can in the back yard. As he walked back up the driveway to the front, he was a little startled to see someone standing on his porch. It was Shelby.

"Hi Jack," she greeted, a big smile on her face.

"Shelby. You scared the daylights out of me."

"Oh. Sorry about that. I was ringing your doorbell and there was no answer. I was about to leave."

"Yeah. I was taking out the trash." Jack walked up the porch steps and unlocked the front door. "Come on up."

The two walked into Jack's apartment and took a seat on the couch. Jack stood up for a moment, walked into the room just passed the kitchen and turned up the thermostat. The furnace hummed for a few seconds and kicked in. Warm air rushed from the vents in the ceiling. He walked back into the living room and took a seat beside Shelby.

"Are you mad at me for looking at those pictures?" she asked.

"I was at first, but thanks to the note that you left, I was able to solve the last bit of this case."

"How so?"

"Well, you mentioned being in a pit lined with sticks. That reminded me of a cradle. Bob Woodring had mentioned something like that. He'd said that the other girls were resting in the cradles that he'd made for them. I knew then that he had buried them. When you went on in your note to say that you had been in a wooden shed, I was reminded of something that Percy Stuart had told me about the property in Greeley Township. He'd said that there was an outbuilding."

"What's an outbuilding?" Shelby asked.

"It's like a shed. Anyway, I found a map of what the Rainey property out in Greeley Township used to look like and from that, I was able to determine where the outbuilding had once stood."

"And where's that?"

"In the backyard of the house that Trish and I had stopped at. The FBI is out there right now conducting a search."

"They are?"

Just then the doorbell rang. Jack stood up and looked out the window. He could see his cousin's car parked in the driveway.

"Speaking of Trish, she's just arrived. I know she's been dying to meet you. I'll be back in a second."

Jack ran down the stairs and to the front door where Trish was waiting on the porch. In her hands, she held a small manila folder. He opened the door and let her in.

"Hi, Jack. How are you doing?"

"Not bad," he replied. "How was the drive?"

"Boring as always." Trish suddenly noticed the stitches on the bridge of Jack's nose. "You know, every time I see you, you have something else wrong with your face."

"I got..."

"No. I don't need to know. I'm sure it's a great story though."

"It is. Well, come on up. There's someone that I want you to meet."

Trish followed Jack up into his place. As they reached the top of the stairs, Shelby stood up as a gesture of courtesy.

"Trish, I'd like you to meet Shelby Tomlinson," Jack introduced. "Shelby, this is my cousin, Trish Martin."

"Hello," Trish warmly greeted.

"It's a pleasure to meet you," replied Shelby.

"Please, have a seat. Both of you."

The ladies took him up on his offer. Shelby resumed her seat on the couch and Trish sat down in a chair. Jack walked around the coffee table and set himself down beside Shelby.

"Jack has told me about all the help that you've given him with my case," Shelby began. "If it weren't for you, he might never have figured it out."

"Well, I was just glad to help."

"And a big help you were," Jack agreed. "Shelby's right. It was the connection between the Rainey House and Bob Woodring that ultimately led me to him. Without that, I doubt that he ever would have been found out."

"I'm sure that you would have eventually figured it out on your own."

"Maybe, but not in time to save Rebecca Lowe." Jack paused for a second as he had suddenly remembered his brief conversation with Trish a few minutes earlier. "Oh, you said that there were a few things that you needed to show me?"

"Yeah," Trish said as she briefly glanced at Shelby. "But I don't think that this is an appropriate time."

"Seems as good a time as any." As soon as Jack said this, his phone began to ring. He looked down at the caller ID and saw that it was Special Agent Spurlock. "If you'll excuse me for a moment." He answered the phone.

"Hi, Drew?"

"Yeah Jack, it's me."

"What's going on?"

"You were right again. We brought out some cadaver-sniffing dogs earlier this evening and they started going nuts so we called in an excavation team and began to dig. We've just uncovered our first set of human remains."

"And are they from a female?"

Shelby and Trish's ears perked up at this.

"Don't know yet. The forensics team is on its way down right now. They should be here at any moment."

"I see."

"Look, Jack. I'll keep you posted on our progress. We never could have gotten this far without your help."

"Thanks, Drew. I appreciate the call. I'll talk to you after while."

Jack hung up the phone and looked over at his two guests who were studying him curiously.

"What was that all about?" Trish asked.

"That was Special Agent Andrew Spurlock of the FBI. They're tearing up that old lady's backyard out in Greeley Township."

"They found something?" asked Shelby.

"Yes. They've discovered a human skeleton, but they're not even sure of the gender yet."

"We all know that it's one of his victims," continued Trish.

"I know. He's going to call me back when they find out more."

There was a long and awkward pause in the conversation. Finally Trish spoke up again.

"We need to go out there."

"Why? There's nothing for us to see."

"Just trust me on this one Jack. We need to be there."

"I seriously doubt that they'll even let us anywhere close."

"Come on. After all that you've done to help them. You

think that they're going to deny you access to the crime scene? It's a crime that you solved."

"Okay. Here's an even better question. Why would *I* want to go out there? You know that sort of thing gives me the creeps."

"Jack. I'm certain that you need to be there." Trish turned to Shelby. "And you need to be there too."

"Me?" Shelby exclaimed.

"Yes. You have to come."

Jack looked over at Shelby. They could both tell that there was no way of getting out of this. It seemed that no matter what they said or did, Trish was going to have her way. They'd just have to play it out.

"Okay," Jack said at last. "We'll go."

The drive out to Greeley Township was quiet and uneventful. Jack tried to start up a couple of conversations, but they fizzled out rather quickly. He'd have thought that Trish would have had a million questions to ask Shelby, as she'd seemed so excited to meet her. As it turned out, Trish didn't seem very interested in her at all. She seemed distant and cold. After about forty-five minutes, they finally pulled into Fleur-de-lis Estates. Jack continued to drive until he came to a barricade. He parked the black Mazda Protegé 5 on the side of the road, stepped out with the other two and proceeded to approach the yellow police line. Trish had her manila folder in her hand. It was very cold outside and Jack was wishing that he could just wait in the car with the heater running.

"I'm sorry, Sir," a police officer said to him, "but you'll have to step back and wait with the others."

Jack looked over and saw that amidst the gathering crowd were many news reporters and cameramen.

"Can you get on the radio and tell Special Agent Andrew Spurlock that Jack Sullivan is here?"

"Agent Spurlock? One second."

The police officer stepped away from them for a moment and talked into his radio. After a few seconds, he came back and lifted the police line for them. They ducked under it and headed for the back yard. Jack looked over and could see Laverne Quinstead standing in her driveway, talking with a couple of FBI agents. She obviously wasn't very happy at the moment.

As they rounded the corner of the house, they could see that a long trench had been dug in the back yard. Floodlights illuminated the scene, bathing the area with an ethereal white glow. On the ground lay a few white sheets. Laid out upon these were what appeared to be three decomposed human corpses. Jack turned to Shelby and Trish.

"You'd better wait here," he told them.

"I have no problem with that," Shelby replied but Trish said nothing.

Jack walked over to the trench were Agent Spurlock had been talking with a member of the forensics team.

"Jack," he began, "you shouldn't have bothered to come out here. I was going to call you at some point and give you an update."

"I know. I guess I just had to see it for myself." Jack needed some excuse. Telling him that he was there because his cousin made him go would sound a bit ridiculous.

"Hoping for some closure? I'm afraid that it takes most people more than this to get over something as horrid as what you've been through. Still, feel free to stick around if you like."

"Thanks. So, have you made any identifications yet?"

"Officially? No. But the first one that we brought up is most likely Anne Perkins. We found her library card in a coat pocket."

"I see. Oh, I also wanted to ask if you had managed to match any of those articles with the girls in the pictures."

"Yeah, a few, but I didn't get very far before you had called and tipped us off about all of this. I'll get back to it soon, but it looks like I'm going to have a full dance ticket for quite some time."

"I'd imagine so. Well, I don't want to get in the way so I'm going to go and stand over there by my cousin."

"Okay. I'll talk to you after while."

Jack walked back over to the corner of the yard where Shelby and Trish were standing.

"I don't know what you brought us out here for," he asked Trish. "He was going to call me with updates."

"And he didn't say anything that sounded odd to you?"

"Not at all. I told him that I came out here looking for closure and he told me that it would probably take more than this."

"He was right, Jack. I seriously doubt that you'll ever get closure."

"How do you mean?"

Just then, a voice called out from down inside of the pit.

"We've got another one here!"

Everyone came in closer to have a look. A couple of people wearing HAZMAT suits jumped down into the pit and began to move the soil around.

"Make that two!" the voice corrected. "Bring us a couple of sheets!"

A federal agent walked over and handed down two folded up white sheets. Another pulled out a camera and began to take photographs. Jack recognized him as Agent Novak, who was in Bob Woodring's barn on Wednesday night. Jack, Shelby and Trish watched as they pulled the first sheet out, set it on the ground and opened it up. The body, though badly decomposed, was still wearing its clothes. It also seemed to be clutching a backpack of some sort.

"I've got more sticks here," announced a voice from within the pit. "What's with this guy and the sticks?"

Agent Spurlock shot a glance over at Jack, certain that he knew something about it. Jack looked over at the sheets with the corpses on them. Something wasn't adding up. There were already four bodies pulled out and they were getting ready to bring up a fifth. There should only have been four. He must have buried another girl from Buffalo here. Jack began to wonder how many more they would find before the night was over.

They started to bring up the next body. The sheet was handed out to the forensics team who set it down on the ground. After it was opened, a woman in an overcoat began to talk into a hand-held digital voice recorder.

"Set number five. Female. Early to mid-teens. Approximately sixty-five inches tall. Wearing boots and a denim jacket. Cause of death unknown. Likely foul play."

She clicked off the recorder and walked back over to the pit. Shelby gazed over at the body with bewilderment.

"I used to have a jacket just like that," she said at last.

"And you still do, Sweetie," Trish told her.

Jack and Shelby gave her a funny look.

"What are you talking about?" Jack asked.

"I'm talking about this." Trish handed him a newspaper article dated from May of 1993. It was the same article that Jack had on the near abduction of Lauren Call.

"Trish, I already have this article."

"Did you read it?"

"Of course I read it."

"And what did you get out of it?"

"It's full of typos and misinformation."

"Look at the bottom."

"Yeah, they misspelled the word 'Ford'."

"Not that. The part about five girls already missing."

"It's a typo."

"No Jack, it isn't." Trish handed him another page. It was a missing person's poster. "Pam sent me copies of the articles that you gave her and I've been doing some research of my own. I looked closely at that article about Lauren Call and went from there."

Jack looked down at the missing person's poster and couldn't believe his eyes.

Missing: Shelby Louise Tomlinson. Female. Age at time of abduction: 14. Brown hair and blue eyes. Five feet, five inches tall. One hundred and ten pounds, at time of abduction. Missing since October 17th 1992. Last seen on Lynnwood Drive in Oakhurst, Ohio wearing blue jeans, brown boots, black tee shirt, white thermal shirt and blue denim jacket with colorful writing on it.

Jack looked closely at the poster. There were now two pictures on it. The first was the one that he had seen the night that he'd first met Shelby. The second was one that made her look somewhat older. The caption beneath it said *"age progression"*. The poster was dated from 1995. He looked up at Shelby who was obviously scared out of her wits. She began to shake her head.

"No, no, no, no, no! It's not true. Say it's not true!"

"I'm sorry, Dear," Trish told her, "but it is true."

"That's not me!" she screamed, pointing at the skeleton in the denim jacket.

"I'm afraid it is."

"No, it isn't!"

"Think about it Shelby. You see Jack almost every night. What do you do when you're not with him?"

"I go home?"

"And what street do you live on?"

"I... I..."

"You don't know, do you? Okay. What's your phone number?"

There was a long pause as Shelby tried to think of it.

"I'm not dead!" she blasted. "Don't you see that? Don't you see that I'm not dead?"

"Of course you're not dead," Trish added. "We can see you."

"Then why are you saying that that's me over there?"

"Because no one ever really dies. We just change is all. That *was* you over there, but it isn't anymore. This is you now."

"So what am I?" Shelby asked through tears.

"There are so many names for it."

"A ghost?"

"That's one, but that's such a broad term."

"Jack, I'm real. You can see me, right?

Jack was completely beside himself. It was as if the sky had just turned green and the grass, blue.

"Yes, Shelby," he said at last, "I can see you."

"So there!" she said turning back to Trish. "I'm not a ghost! Jack can see me!"

"Yeah, I'm still trying to figure out why that is," Trish continued with a slight look of bewilderment on her face. "I kind of always knew that he might have the gift, but wasn't completely certain."

"But I can touch him! I'm real. Watch!" Shelby ran up and gave Jack a big embrace. His head started to spin and he felt as though he were going to fall over. "You see?"

"Jack, how do you feel?" Trish asked.

"A bit woozy, but I can feel her."

"I told you so!" Shelby shouted.

"That is interesting," Trish continued.

"So what? Do I have the same gift as you then?" Jack asked as he tried to regain his composure.

"Close, but I have a feeling that Shelby is the only spirit that you'll ever see."

"Why is that?"

"I don't know, Jack. I'm not a fortuneteller. Maybe you two were supposed to end up together. If this guy hadn't come along and taken her life, who knows what might have happened? I have no idea what fate originally had planned for you. I can tell you this; your destinies are somehow connected."

"But if she died when she was fourteen, why does she look like she's in her late twenties?"

"Like I just told her, she's not dead, only changed. She continued to grow up and do the things that she otherwise would never have had the chance to do."

"Like go to college and become a veterinarian?"

"Exactly."

"But none of that ever really happened."

"It happened to her, therefore it's real."

"But she remembers escaping from the outbuilding and being found in the woods a few miles her house."

"She did escape. Well, her soul did anyway. The rest of it was what she wanted to happen, so it did. She just forgot about the part where he strangled her."

"Where he what?" Shelby asked with a look of shock on her face.

"He strangled you, Sweetie, and threw you into that pit," Trish continued.

Shelby found it hard to breathe and wondered if in fact she really was.

"Isn't this the point where she should be seeing a light or something and moving on?" Jack asked.

"You've seen too many movies. A light doesn't necessarily come for everyone. Not right away, at least."

"But I thought that it all had to do with unfinished business and that sort of thing."

"That's mostly Hollywood stuff, Jack."

"But she's free now."

"Maybe she's just not ready to leave."

Jack looked over at Shelby who was now sobbing uncontrollably. He walked over and tried to console her.

"It's alright," he whispered. "You're not alone in this."

"Easy for you to say," she said through a sniffle. "You're not the one who's dead!"

"Neither are you, remember?"

"Yeah! Well what do you call that?" she shouted, pointing at her corpse.

"Sweetie," Trish broke in. "What you're going through right now is completely natural. We'll all have to face it at some point. That's the order of things. Count your blessings though. You have Jack. Most people have no one and have to face this alone."

Shelby dried her eyes and threw herself at Jack, wrapping her arms around him. Jack fought off the urge to fall over.

"We should really get going," Trish told them.

"Can I have a moment?" Shelby asked.

"Sure."

Shelby walked over to where her decomposing body lay on the sheet. She stared at it for a few minutes not quite knowing what to think. At long last, she gave a shudder and sobbed. She glanced back over at Jack and Trish who were patiently waiting for her, then looked up into the sky. For a moment, she thought that she saw a star begin to twinkle in a funny way. The manner in which it shimmered made her feel more relaxed. Gradually, the light from this star began to intensify and she started to hear a strange hissing noise that seemed to build in volume and pitch. The light grew brighter and her whole body began to tingle. The experience terrified her beyond anything that she ever though could. Quickly, she looked away from the star and shook her head vigorously until the hissing noise subsided and was completely gone.

After regaining her composure, she walked back over to Jack and Trish.

"What just happened to me?" she asked Trish, who seemed to be more knowledgeable of such matters.

"That," Trish replied, "I think, was the light."

"Why was it so scary?"

"The unknown is a scary thing. We naturally fear what we don't understand."

"So I missed it then?"

"For now, but I'm sure that you'll see it again."

"So what do I do now?"

At first, Jack and Trish had no answer for her. After a moment, Jack spoke up.

"You could always come back with us."

Shelby closed her eyes and considered the offer. At length, she began to nod.

"Then we should get going," Trish suggested. "There really isn't anything more for us here to see."

With that, the three of them found their way back to Jack's car, got in and made the long drive back to Lakewood. It was a quiet ride.

No one said a word.

Chapter 24

Shelby Tomlinson was 14 years old when she was abducted on the night of October 17th 1992 while walking home from her friend Jayna's house. For two weeks, she had been chained up and sexually assaulted in the basement of a house located at 4021 Indianola Road in Greeley Township, Ohio. Her life was ended on the night of October 31st when her abductor, a man named Robert Marshall Woodring, strangled her to death. He carried her lifeless body outside, past the barn and into an outbuilding. There, he laid her down in a deep pit that he'd lined with sticks. She had made so much noise, the little baby, so he decided to put her to sleep and lay her down in a cradle that he'd built just for her. Here she could rest and always be his perfect little angel. He needed more though, and there were plenty of others out there. If they would make too much noise and cry, he'd put them to sleep as well. After many years of this, he had accumulated quite a collection: his little babies, resting all across the country. As long as no one found them and woke them up, they would be his forever, always asleep… in the cold, cradled ground.

Jack had a daunting task ahead of him. After analyzing the drawings on the walls and the photographs found in Bob Woodring's desk, he and Agent Spurlock concluded that there were thirty-nine victims in all. Worse yet was that they were scattered across eight different states. Five had recently been discovered in the greater Cleveland area, which left thirty-four in seven more states. Jack was determined to find them all and set them free. They could no longer be Bob Woodring's sleeping little angels.

Jack sat at his desk that cold and bright Saturday morning in early November looking over the pictures of the walls that Agent Spurlock had given him. He keyed on the photos of the drawings that contained boxes and numbers. He'd figured out what these meant and was trying to match the property layouts with the pictures of the houses. It was a difficult task, but he'd already made a couple of matches. He still had no idea where these houses were located. He'd have to take it one step at a time.

As he leaned back in his chair and stretched out his arms, Jack glanced over to where Shelby Tomlinson was lying down, asleep on his couch. She had stayed the entire night with him. He didn't know what to think about her at this point. What was she? A ghost? A spirit? A poltergeist? Maybe residual energy left behind from when her life was tragically cut short. He had no idea. She was 29 years old now and had grown up in her own way, with her own memories. Who was he, Jack thought, to question any of that. Still, whatever she was, she was there and she was with him. He took some comfort in this.

To track down and set free all of these girls that Bob Woodring had murdered would be a long and arduous journey. Jack was definitely up to the challenge. It was beginning to look more and more like his cousin Trish was right.

He never would get over this case.